KATHI S. BARTON

This is a work of fiction. Names, characters, places, and incidents are products of the author's imagination or are used fictitiously and are not to be construed as real. Any resemblance to actual events, locations, organizations, or persons, living or dead, is entirely coincidental.

World Castle Publishing, LLC
Pensacola, Florida

Paperback ISBN: 9781949812794
eBook ISBN: 9781949812800
First Edition World Castle Publishing, LLC, March 18, 2019
http://www.worldcastlepublishing.com

Licensing Notes

Cover: Karen Fuller
Editor: Maxine Bringenberg

Chapter 1

Angus came to her with every little thing, Mason thought. So much so that she wanted to brain him. But she supposed that was a good idea until he was more comfortable with his new position as the front man for a place they were going to work with. Mason loved him, and that was all she needed to let things roll off her with this transfer of power. At least for the time being, it would be good for him to get answers before making a commitment. He'd make a good replacement for her at Mason Tile and Paper.

Her brother was doing much better than she'd thought he would in so little time. Mason was getting closer and closer to her time to run away. Not that it was really what she was doing, but her dad and brother thought that she was. And while they weren't wrong about her leaving the firm, they weren't right either. Mason Jane Barnhart had had enough of things in general. She also knew what no one else did—that she didn't have long to live.

For two days now, she'd been out walking about the tiny town. It was small compared to where she'd lived most of her life. Chicago was a nice town, one that she loved, but that too had been too much for her in dealing with everything. Everyone, even in a town as big as hers, had heard something about what had happened to her. Not all of it, but enough to ask her if she was doing all right. And at least daily, someone asked her about her health and wellbeing.

No, she thought to herself. She was not doing all right. But she would only smile at them and nod. Yes, Mason would say, I'm doing just fine. I'm over it. And that had to be the biggest lie she'd ever told anyone, especially her family.

Not that either of them knew much of what had happened to her. Nor did they know the extent of her injuries that she carried to this day. Not just the emotional ones, but the ones that were on her flesh, so that each day she was sure it was going to be her last. And hiding it from her family and friends was taking its toll on her. She was going to die. A long and painful death that would not only drain her father's business, but also his health by staying at her side.

Mason stopped by the little bridge she'd walked by a dozen times over the last few weeks. The first day she'd been by it had been a dry and sunny day. The water, not all that deep, was babbling around the low hanging trees, as well as the large stones in the waterway. The fallen trees that no doubt came from upstream formed cascading water sounds that had made her smile despite the circumstances surrounding her interest in the water. Then it started to rain, a deluge of water that seemed to have been an open spigot on the town and all the now swollen creeks. This was just what she was looking for in a way to end her life by falling to her death.

Mason knew that drowning wasn't a sure thing when it came to jumping into the fast running creek. But she'd been coming by here at its lower point, and saw that there was a great big stone in the middle of the waterway. And if her estimations were correct, the fast-moving water was just about freezing. There were icy formations along both sides where the water didn't move as fast.

Sitting on the railing, her feet dangling over the water, she wondered what the impact would be for her to fall directly on the large stone that had made its way above the moving water. It was a creek, she'd been told, that fed into the Muskingum River downstream from where they were. A long way to go, she thought, before anyone would realize that she'd jumped.

"Hello." She didn't bother to look at the man. She'd seen him around town too. Actually, it was difficult to go into any place on the main drag without seeing Mr. Whitfield—Oliver, he'd asked Angus to call him. "Are you going to jump?"

"I've not decided just yet. I was calculating in my head how hard the water would be, and the stone beneath it." She looked at him then. "I have a lot on my mind, Mr. Whitfield. I thank you for your concern. However, this is nothing that I'd like to share with a stranger. It's a place I come to think, and I'd like to do that alone, if you'd not mind."

"Yes, I can understand that. I'm Oliver Whitfield. If I'm not mistaken, you're one of the workers that is with Angus. Good fella, by the way. I think he has a brother hereabouts, but I've not had the pleasure of meeting him just yet. Honey, is there anything I can do to help you?" It was on the tip of her tongue to ask him if he would push her into certain death, but she didn't. Instead, she just looked out over the muddy, icy water. "I have a couple of doctors in my family. They'd be more than happy to talk to you, child."

"Do you have a gun, Mr. Whitfield?" He said that he didn't. Realizing her mistake, she had to think fast about telling him why she'd needed a gun. "Then no, I don't think there is a thing you can do for me. I was...there are a few snakes here and about in the water. I was going to practice on them. I have a permit to carry, but I don't. Not anymore."

"I don't mean to be rude, and my lovely wife would box my ears for this, but I don't believe that you want a gun for that at all. Can you tell me about it? I promise you on my wife's heart that I'd never tell anyone else." Mason shook her head. "I need for you to tell me what's bothering you, child. I'm not leaving here until you do."

"At the moment, you're the only thing bothering me, Mr. Whitfield. As I said, I have a few things I need to work out on my own." He sat on the side of the bridge with her, his jean covered legs and high boots looking ridiculous next to her fancy worthless boots and lightweight pants. "Mr. Whitfield, I'd very much like for you to go away and leave me alone. I'm not going to share anything with you. There isn't anything you can do, and even if there was, I don't want anyone to be a part of this."

"This here creek, did you know that it's called Narrows Creek? Been here since the man over there decided to widen his fields so that he didn't have to cross a little bitty bridge in the spring when the creek flooded. And boy oh boy, it sure could flood." She looked at the house that was on the other side of the field, but said nothing. "That's his home, if you're thinking that. He's not lost anything since he had some people come in and widen and deepen this place for him. Don't jump."

Tears filled her eyes. The man was too smart for her own good. He was much too observant as well. Instead of answering him, even though she wouldn't, she thought of what he'd said about Angus having a brother.

"Angus doesn't have a brother, Mr. Whitfield. I'm his

sister, Mason." She looked at him. "Mas Barnhart is our father. Not really Angus's, but he is mine. Dad bought me off my mother so that she'd not abort me when she found out that she was knocked up. Not a good term, I guess, but those were her words, not his. Then a few months after I was born, no more than an infant, she was killed in an automobile accident." She hadn't expected him to say anything, so when he didn't, she continued. "Angus's mother thought that she'd get a great deal of money from my dad by claiming that my dad was the father of him. He wasn't, of course, but that didn't stop him from paying her off, and he still does when she shows up making a stink about shit that isn't true, nor any of her business. Mostly, lately anyway, the shit has been about me."

"You seem like a good girl. What on earth could she have on a child like you?"

She just stared at the creek, watching it roar along the sides of the banks, pulling limbs and leaves along with it to make pretty colored swirls in the waterway as it flowed downstream. Trees, too, had been moved, probably a great distance, and were starting to pile up at the posts that held the bridge she and Mr. Whitfield were sitting on.

"Mason, what happened to you?"

"A man did. Not that you'd have to believe me or not. Frankly, I don't have any proof at all that he even touched me that week. But he kidnapped me from campus where I was teaching, drugged me, and raped me, repeatedly, over an entire week and then some. There were others too. All men, who I found out later had paid a great deal of money to have their way with me." She laughed bitterly, not even sure why she was sharing this with him. A last confession, she thought, because she was going to jump today. "I was the great Mas

Barnhart's daughter, his princess that was so untouchable. I haven't any idea where that had come from, but there it was. And lucky for me, or not so lucky for me, I was able to escape with my life. Or so I thought."

She looked at Mr. Whitfield. He had a kind face, one that she thought reminded her a great deal of her own father. She knew this man had sons, six of them. And he had grandchildren and a nice wife. Carefully she reached out her hand, meaning only to touch his cheek to see if it felt as soft and warm as she thought it might. But curling her fingers into her palm at the last minute, she thanked him for being there.

The jump was easy. Mason just stood and leapt. But she wasn't getting to the water as she had hoped—something was keeping her there. Turning her head to look at Mr. Whitfield, she saw that he was holding her back by her coat, and his grip was too powerful for her to shake loose. Mason did try to make him release her so that she'd not have to come back another day to try again. This was her last chance, she thought, and she needed it to work.

"Don't do it, child. We can work something out." She reached for the zipper on her coat, pulling it down slowly as Mr. Whitfield strained to hold her back. She wanted to just rip it off, let him have the coat that he was holding so that she could die. But the strain on it and her body was making it go slowly. "Please, I'm begging of you, child, don't do this. There has to be another way."

"There isn't."

The coat was undone and she let it slip from her arms. The water came up fast, and Mason closed her eyes for the impact. Hoping that it would kill her right away, she let out a breath that she'd been holding, and hit the water hard.

She had missed the stone except for her arm. The water

was so cold that it made her inhale sharply. The pain of it, like icy needles, felt as if it were tearing her flesh from her body. Mason didn't care. She was going to be free soon, and that was all that mattered. Not fighting the current or the trees that banged into her, she let it take her under several times as she tried to get her bearings on where she was in the water.

The water was rough, tumbling and turning her all around so that she didn't know which way was up. Bashing her body off one thing to the next, she knew that her arm and leg were broken, useless to her in trying to hold herself under. And when she knocked her shoulder, the pain of it making her cry out, she swallowed more water, then nothing. The pain in her head took it all away.

~*~

Oliver had put out an emergency call for help when Mason stood up. He'd been talking to Evan since seeing her there, but he never dreamed in a million years that she'd do it right in front of him. Shifting to his tiger, he dove into the water after her, knowing that his cat would stand the cold a bit better than he would as a man.

He had a difficult time finding her in the murky water. He'd see her for a second, but then she was gone. Oliver knew that they were farther down the creek than he'd told his family, but there wasn't any time for him to get his bearings and find the girl. As soon as he had a good hold on her leg, he bit down hard, knowing that if he lost her this time, he'd never have a second chance of finding her again. The bones, already broken, shattered more under his powerful bite.

"Dad, can you see me? Dad, I'm here." He popped his head above the water in time to hear Evan yelling for him. "Christ, bring her to me and I'll see what I can do. They're all coming, Dad. We'll save her if we can."

Oliver swam as hard as he could to get to the other side, but he was an old man, worn out by hard work and age. Oliver wasn't giving up, but he knew that he wasn't going to make it to his son. Then he felt his burden become lighter and looked to his other son. Josh had come into the water as his cat to help him.

It was a struggle, even for the two of them, to get her to Evan. As soon as his son was able to reach into the water and pull her out, Josh got out as well and helped him out of the freezing cold water. Oliver didn't have the strength to shift—he wasn't even sure that he had the energy to breathe. But his lovely wife, the woman of his heart, Eve, yelled at him through their link. While he'd never tell her this, she sounded like a choir of angels talking to him.

You die there on the side of that nasty creek, Oliver Whitfield, and I will never forgive you. I won't visit your grave, nor will I put any pretties there for you. Get up, you old coot, and move around before you freeze to death. He told her that he loved her. *I love you too. And you were so brave to save her. Now, you'd better be up and around before I get there. Or so help me I'll—*

I'm up. Now hush, woman, I can't hear what Evan is saying about her. It might have been for nothing. Evan was looking grave as he worked. Then he looked at him. *She's got some kind of sickness, Evan. I tasted it in her blood when I bit her.*

"You're going to have to finish the job, Dad, or she will be dead before I can do a thing." He asked him what he was talking about. "Change her. You've bitten her several times, it looks like. And she's dying. Change her and she'll live. And it'll take care of whatever illness brought her to this point. As it is right now, she's got so many broken bones, and with the loss of blood, I don't know if she'd make it even if this were to have happened with a team of doctors around her. Change her, please."

He didn't want to. Oliver wasn't sure why, but he had a feeling that this little girl was going to be one of his sons' mate. Evan told him it was now or she'd be dead to someone. He bit down in her bruised and battered belly, and felt her scream that came up from her gut. She was poisoned with something nasty, the poor thing, and he had a feeling that she'd been right. Mason had been about as close to death as it came.

It was another twenty minutes before he could move away from her tiny body. Ivy was there with them now, and so was his Eve, who had brought him some clothing. When Mason started to shake hard, they covered her with as many blankets and coats as they could find. All it did, he thought, was make her shake harder. It wasn't until Carter showed up that he could see some improvement in her skin. But she gave her a couple of drops of her powerful blood to be sure.

They all knew that Carter was a fae, and that she had shared her magic with Josh. But what it would do to a human, one that was just on this side of dying, no one knew. It might well be a moot point if she died right now.

It was decided, however, that they'd take her up to the bridge and lay her down there, so that when the ambulance came, they'd just say that she had slipped on the icy bridge. It was plausible, he supposed. She was soaking wet and badly battered. Carter said she'd make it, so the authorities saw only what they needed to see, and he was grateful for that.

"Her brother and dad, they don't need to know that she was trying to kill herself." Eve agreed, but Evan wasn't so sure. "If he needs to know, then we'll tell him. But I think, for now, we should just let it go as a fall rather than her jumping. I think this is something that she'll need to tell them. On her terms, I think, too. I'd want to hear it from one of you if you were thinking there wasn't any other way."

"What about changing her?" Oliver told Evan he didn't know about that yet as he pulled off his second coat to lay on Mason, to make it look as if he'd been the only one there. "All right. But think on an answer or something before we get in too deep with this. Her dad, he might even know that she's been down of late. But I doubt very much that he knew that she was dying with what she had. That is more than likely what drove her here in the first place."

He had to agree. But he'd not tell any of them what she'd said to him before she'd jumped. It tore at his heart when he thought of the sadness and pain that he'd seen there just before she slipped out of her coat.

The ambulance was called, and he waited for them. The rest of them left him there so that the story was plausible. He held her hand while he sat there with her, telling her that it mattered little to him if she was one of his boys' mate, he already loved her to pieces.

When the ambulance pulled up, Ivy was on it with them. With a wink at him, she asked him what was going on. He told her the story that they'd agreed on. He'd found her there, lying on the bridge, and had covered her up with his coat. He didn't have to explain why she was wet, no one asked, but once she was bundled up and taken away, Oliver sat there for a few more minutes, thinking of his part in this woman's life now.

He'd not changed anyone in his life. Not even when he'd been younger had he had the occasion to do something so terrifying. His lady wife, Eve, had been a full-blooded tiger when they'd come together. And now, he'd just changed the life of someone, a stranger, so profoundly that he doubted very much she'd ever be able to forgive him. Oliver wasn't sure that he'd ever forgive himself if it came to that. But she was alive, and she'd be all right. Oliver thought that was the best he could be happy for right now.

"Are you finished feeling sorry for yourself?" He turned to look at Tanner when he spoke. "You saved her life, at great risk to yourself. And while she might have wanted to die, by her own hand, you have done something wonderful for her family. As you thought, she might not forgive you right away. But Oliver, I have known you all my life, and no one can be upset with you for long."

"I'm not like my father." He looked around and saw that it had turned rainy again, the clouds thick and heavy. "He could charm the pants off a nun, I've been told. By him, mostly, but I have heard it. I'm not the type of person that can make anyone do anything."

"Let me see your arm." Oliver had hurt himself holding the girl so she'd not fall. It had just begun to hurt him when Tanner sat beside him on the cold, wet bridge. "You strained it badly, I'm afraid. You will need to be in more pain before you will be better. I would have thought that shifting to catch her would have helped."

"My cat was hurt. The current that had us, it was much stronger than I'd thought when I went in for her." He looked at Tanner. "She was dying. I just couldn't let her do that to herself. Or her family. She is better now, I'm hoping. Do you think you can do that magical thing you do and tell me if I did a worse thing by doing this to her?"

"I shan't do that, Oliver. You know as well as I that she will live for a good long time now, and have no worries that she had before." Oliver nodded, but wasn't convinced that she'd not try again. "She will not. I shall tell you something, my friend. She is the mate to one of your sons, but I know not which one. And that alone will give her immortality, regardless of her being the wonderful tiger that I know she will be."

"Do you know this man? The one that she was talking about before she jumped?" He said that he didn't. "I wish I did. I'd hunt him down and give him a good showing of my cat. Even as old as I am, I think I could make him wet himself."

"Don't do it, my friend. While I have no doubt that you could make him wet his pants, I think you should leave that for your son, her mate. But as I have said, you will need to see Ivy or Evan about your arm. I believe that you have dislocated your shoulder. Quite painful, I have heard, so you will, as I said, be in a great deal more pain." Tanner stood up. "I wish to ask you something, Oliver, and you do not need to form an answer. And though I am quite aware of what you are going to say, I wish for you to think on it. Her father, I have heard, is a good man. What would you feel should this have been your despondent child, and a man—you, in this case—had the chance to save her from certain death, so changed her into something more? How would you feel?"

Tanner disappeared, not waiting to see if Oliver had an answer or not. The sun was coming out and the rain was gone. The roads, he knew, would be slicker before dinner tonight. Walking home, enjoying the chill of the day, he thought about the question that had been put before him.

"I'd want her to be alive more than anything." He knew that to be true, but he also didn't know the other man, her father. His dad did, of course. Dad knew everyone. But Oliver didn't.

Making his way to the diner, Oliver decided to have a talk with his dad about it.

"So you saved her life." Dad was talking to him between customers. Oliver had an idea that he needed something to do like his dad had, if only to make him feel better about life. Dad sure did look better than he had a few months ago. "I know Mas. He's a good man, and a better businessman than I've come across. If he has his little girl, then you can bet that he wouldn't care if she was a donkey braying out her love for him."

"Dad, where do you come up with this stuff? There has to be a place that has a list of them. Every day you come up with something new, and just as goofy." Dad laughed when he did. "I heard that the boys are going to be helping him out so that no one takes his company. It's good to see someone still doing business within the family."

"It is, I agree. And if'n you want me to, I'll be there when you tell him what you did to his little girl. I didn't know that— Say, you thinking what I'm thinking?" Oliver told him that he was still thinking about that girl braying like a jackass. "I never said jackass, you dummy. I said a donkey. But what if she's one of the boys' mates? Wouldn't that be a hoot?"

"It might be if I wasn't so afraid that she isn't." Dad asked him why. "Because she's a tiger, Dad. She's no longer a human." He didn't tell him what Tanner had said. For some reason he wanted to keep that to himself for now.

"Oh, don't go on about that. Whoever she's mated to, you can bet your bottom pocket lint that this other person is going to be a durn sight happier with her being alive, don't you think?" Amazed at his father's sayings, Oliver just nodded. "There you go. And if she happens to be one of them boys' mates, well, you had it right on to make her something that could be running with him. Don't go looking for trouble, Oliver. You don't need to. Trust me when I tell you, when it comes around, this here trouble that's in your head, it'll find you without you worrying yourself sick over it. Now, have some pie, then go on over and get that bum arm looked at. I can see that it hurts you."

He walked over to the clinic after having a slice of pie with his dad. Oliver was glad to see that one of the other doctors was there today. Oliver knew that Evan was on call and Ivy had taken Mason in, so he'd not be embarrassed when someone set his arm for him. The man told him the same thing that Tanner had—it was going to be more painful before it started to get better.

Once they strapped him to the table, really making him more nervous than before, he laid there just thinking about the woman, trying his best not to think of her as a girl. Calling her one when he could see that she wasn't, Oliver hoped that she'd be all right.

"I came by when I heard from Tanner. Oh, Oliver, I wish you could have said something. I would have picked you up." Oliver was happy to see Eve—so happy, in fact, that he held her hand when the doctor came into the room. "You just lay there and let him fix you up. Then I'll take you home and pamper you for a bit. I think there is even a little pie left over from dinner last night."

There wasn't any pie—he'd had it before leaving the house this morning. But he'd not tell her. She's be fussy with him again. And right now, he wanted her to be loving and comforting.

The doctor grabbed his arm at the elbow, and all Oliver remembered after that was screaming his fool head off.

Chapter 2

Adrian was working on his speech when he felt his father's pain. Standing up, his phone rang just as he was grabbing up his coat. It was his mom. Sitting down, he waited for her to stop laughing, of all things, before she could speak.

"He's fine. I was going to talk to you all at once, but he's just lying there knocked out, and I had to.... Oh my, Adrian, he's just fine, but I have to tell you, I've never heard him curse like he did just before he passed out." Adrian asked what had happened. "He dislocated his shoulder is all I got from him before he was knocked out from the pain. I think he might have done it when he was saving that young lady. She was in a terrible mess, and your father saved her life."

"Wow, really? What happened, Mom?" She told him what she'd gotten from the others. "I feel so badly for her. Does she have family?"

"Yes, she's the daughter of Mason Barnhart. You know the man; his family is working on the hotel." He said that he thought it was two sons. "I guess not. But her name is Mason, so that might have been the confusion. She and your dad had a long conversation, and I guess he was worried about her. When she jumped, I guess it was all he could do to hold onto her, and she still fell in. That's all I know."

"Does Dad need me to come there and help him home? I know you can do it on your own, but you know how he can be about being manly when he's hurt." She laughed again and told him she had him. "All right, Mom. I'm here if you need me."

"I do. Need you, I mean. It's a great deal to ask of you, but could you go and see her? The girl? I guess that Blake saw her when she was brought in—I'm not sure of the details about it—but would you please, for me, go and see if she's your mate?" Adrian felt his heart beat a little harder and his breaths take on a whole new level of breathing hard. "Adrian, are you all right?"

"Yes. I'm fine. She wasn't his mate?" Mom told him that it didn't look like she was. "And you think she's mine for some reason."

"No, that's not it at all, young man." He realized that his voice had taken a hard turn. "Your dad saved her life by changing her into a tiger, and he's a little upset and frightened that someone will take him to task about it. I was just hoping it would ease his mind a little if he knew that he'd done it for one of you. But don't bother with it. I guess we'll just let her go back to her home and heal there."

The phone was disconnected, and Adrian felt it like she'd slammed his heart closed. Putting his phone down, he thought about having a mate. Now. Not only didn't he have time for one, but one that would leap off a bridge to end her life wasn't someone that he thought would look good on his arm when he was elected to his next level.

Getting up, pulling on his suit coat, he told Lily that he'd be back. She was so deep in his campaign work that all she did was wave him off. She was trying to get donations. Why, he had no idea. He could have easily paid for it himself, but according to his brother, that would be a huge mistake. He thought that begging people for money was a mistake, but Adrian went with the flow.

The hospital was busy, and he had to wait his turn before he could speak to Evan or Ivy. They were both busy, he was told, but they would get to him soon. He didn't want to be a bother, but he knew that he had to do some major making up to his mom. Damn it, why did having a mate seem to be the all wonderful to everyone but him?

Adrian wasn't unhappy about having a mate—he didn't care one way or the other. There were lots of single people in the government pool. Hell, even Henry wasn't married. Of course, he had been when he took office the first time, but it didn't seem to hurt his chances by being single the second time he'd been elected.

But a woman that had tried to kill herself? He'd to keep an eye on her at all times so that she'd not try again. Once he met her, he wondered if he could get her help under the radar. Adrian didn't want to ruin his chances of making it to the big house because someone found out that he had a deranged wife.

Knowing that he was being cruel, he saw his brother coming toward him. Adrian didn't know his brother Josh was there, and put out his hand to shake his. But almost as soon as he put his hand around his, Adrian knew that he'd done something wrong by coming here. And when Josh leaned in to whisper to him near his ear, Adrian was sick with the pain his brother was causing him by squeezing his hand so tightly, he was sure that bones were crushing.

"You mother fucker, what makes you think that she's deranged?" Adrian had forgotten about the mind reading thing. "I hope that she is your mate, just so I can see you fail at something once in your life. She's not deranged, dumbass, but depressed. If we were anywhere but in a public place, I'd wipe your fucking ass all over the floor."

"I'm sorry." Josh squeezed his hand once more before stepping back from him. Adrian told him again how sorry he was. Shaking his hand, trying to get the blood flowing again, he looked at his brother. "I'm under a great deal of pressure here. Not that that should be an excuse, but I'm worried about her wellbeing and me running for the house."

"And you don't think that someone deciding to end their life her way instead of what was going to happen to her would have been any less pressure? She was going to die anyway, she thought, but her way, drowning in a fucking creek, was much better and humane. It would have been less suffering for her family was her way of thinking." Josh told him why she was killing herself, about the blood disease she had. "Some dick picked her up and drugged her. Then he let every man he knew that had the same blood disease fuck her until she finally escaped. She spent nine days, nine horrific days, with those men before she was able to get away. Then the poor girl had to run into the woods, half naked, to flag down someone to help her to the hospital. However, just six weeks later, they told her that she was going to die, and that she should get her house in order."

"I'm sorry." Josh waved him off as he started to walk away. "Don't, Josh, please. I'm truly sorry. I shouldn't have said or even thought such horrible things. Even if she might not be my mate, I still should have kept my thoughts like that out of the equation."

"Yes, you should have. Can you imagine what Dad went through? Watching her jump, and all he could do was hold onto her for a moment before she plunged forward." Adrian told him what Mom had told him about Dad. "Yes, his cat knocked his shoulder out of whack, and even with that, he walked to the diner to talk to his dad, then to the clinic. And here you are, whining about how she's going to look hanging on your fucking arm."

He let him walk away this time. Adrian thought that he could have been mad, that his brother had intruded on his thoughts and that wasn't right. But Adrian had been beyond mean, thinking of only himself and not whoever this woman was. If she wasn't his mate, then he still shouldn't have whined, just as Josh said that he had, but had better care with his thoughts and his actions. For he was only here because his mom had guilted him into it.

Finding her room on the fourth floor, he wasn't sure why she was in a regular room rather than the psych ward, but it hadn't been his call. And he knew that he didn't have all the information that he needed to make that sort of decision anyway. Since he didn't have any real answers for that, he decided to keep his opinions to himself. Or better yet, he told himself, not to have any.

As soon as he got into the room, he could smell the blood and other medications that had been given to her. She wasn't alone, even though she was still out, so Adrian, putting his best foot forward, put his hand out to the other man.

"I just heard about Mason's accident." He just then remembered what he'd been told about her reasons for being wet and on the bridge. "I came by to see if you have everything that you need."

"Yes." The man looked over at him. Adrian just

remembered that his name was Angus, son to Mas Barnhart. "Mr. Whitfield, correct?"

"Yes. Call me Adrian." The man said that he looked a great deal like his brothers. "You should see my dad and grandda. You'd think that we're younger versions of them. I came by to see if there was anything I could do for you and your sister. My dad is the one that found her on the bridge with the broken leg and arm."

"I'm just waiting for my dad to get here. He's upset, and no matter how many times I've reassured him that she's right here with me, he still needs to see her. I'm kind of glad that he's coming. Dad can be calming when something is going on." Adrian asked if he could wait with him. "Of course. It's nice to have the company, really. Are you one of the owners of the hotel?"

"My brothers are." He nodded. "I'm to understand that you are happy with what was left behind when it was closed up. When I was younger, my brothers and I used to sneak into the place and ride down the banister."

"I've been tempted a little to do that myself. And yes, very happy. There is an oak desk that must have been made in the place. The bannister, oak as well, is nearly thirty feet long, with all the work in it that one would expect from a hotel as old as this one. I think we have a lot we can do to it to bring out not just the beauty, but the charm of it as well." Angus leaned back in the chair. "Well, are you her mate? Blake, he was in earlier, and he told me that his mom sent him by to see. I don't care one way or the other, but I would like to see Mason happy. She hasn't been for a long time."

"I don't know yet. The room, it's very stuffy with everything that they're giving her. Also, there are the people that have touched her. I just don't know yet." Angus said that he could understand that. "Would you mind very much if I were to sniff her neck? I'd have to get close to her to do that."

"No, go ahead. I love Mason very much, and I do want her happy. She's been the best sister to me since I came to this family. I think that having someone with her all the time will be good for her. Of course, she won't think so. She has to do it all on her own, all the time."

Adrian would know about that. If she was anything like the other women in his family, she was going to be hell on wheels, as his grandda was so fond of saying.

Going to the bed, he leaned in slowly to her throat. He knew the moment that he bent at the waist that she was his, but he needed more from her—to calm his cat, he told himself. But she was hurt, and they both knew it. So, touching his nose to her cheek, Adrian licked her throat and moaned at the taste of her as it hit every one of his taste buds.

"She's yours, isn't she?" Adrian staggered to his seat, telling Angus that she was. "I thought so. I'm glad that it's you. I think you can make her laugh again."

Adrian sat there for several seconds, letting her taste and smell race over his system. His cat was happy too. She was theirs, and she was a cat. Adrian looked at Angus when he realized what he'd said.

"I'm sorry. How did you come up with the thought that I'd be funny?" He said that he'd seen his speech on television the other day, and when he'd taken down the governor of the town. "He was an idiot. And didn't get any smarter in prison, I'm afraid."

"See, right there. That to me is funny. You could have gone on and on about how you'd taken him down, how you'd just found the information, all by yourself. But you didn't. You just stated the fact and didn't tell me a bunch of lies."

Angus smiled at him as he continued. "There is this man that my dad used to work with. He'd come by the house when I was there, and he'd tell Dad how they could make a killing on the market by selling used bricks. Dad turned him down, so he found someone else to go in with him. It wasn't as easy as all that, but you understand. Then about a year later, he came by again, telling my dad how he'd done this and that, how he was a millionaire and all this other crap. Dad just sat there, saying nothing. Not six months later, the man and his partner were in prison because they'd stolen the bricks they were selling off of land they didn't own. And it just happened to be government property that they'd taken them from. Dad never said that he'd tried to warn him, which he had told him to be careful of that sort of thing. Never called up and bragged to whomever would listen how he'd been right. Whenever anyone would bring it up, Dad would just listen and nod, acting as if he didn't know anything about it. I love him for that. I have a feeling that you'd be like that. Not a bragger, but someone that would happily share, if not give all the credit to others around him."

They talked about the new hotel that was being worked on by his firm. Adrian told him about his bid to get in the senate. He enjoyed the conversation, and had to remind himself several times that this man would be his brother-in-law, that they'd be related. He didn't say, even to himself, that it would be soon, but he did think a lot about Mason too.

When Angus asked if he'd stay while he went to stretch his legs, Adrian told him that would be fine. Right now, he supposed that he had nothing better to do than to make sure that his mate didn't need anything. Adrian was very proud of himself for not asking for tidbits about Mason from her brother. He wanted to get to know her on his own.

Reaching out to his mom, he told her he was sorry. *I shouldn't let things build up and then take them out on you and Josh. I'm so very sorry.* She huffed at him. And even through their link, he could feel her disappointment in him. *I'm not looking for you to tell me that I can do this, but I think that I'm in over my head with what I'm trying to do. Not even talking about the White House, but all of it.*

Of course you are. You need to delegate, Adrian. And in that I mean, you need to ask for some help. You have a very large family, and a great many friends around. Ask them to give you a hand. He said that he was going to do that, starting as soon as he got back to the office. *I have your father home now. He's in a great deal of pain, but I think once he sleeps for a bit, he'll feel much better. I heard that Josh told you off. Have you seen the young lady yet?*

Yes. She's my mate. There was silence at the other end of the connection. *I've been talking to her brother. Angus told me that he was glad it was me that was her mate, because I could make her laugh. I don't think I've laughed myself in a good long time. Mom, are you there?*

Yes. I'm trying my best not to get too excited about this, for fear that you're telling me this to make me not mad at you again. He said that he wasn't. *Mason is your mate – you're sure, Adrian?*

Very much so. Then the happiness started to come through to him. Adrian smiled, and wondered what had been going through her head to think that he'd say that to her. But he did want to get on her good side. *I'm here with her now. She's resting. Angus said her dad was on the way, and he went out to stretch his legs. I'm going to contact Dylan and Carter next, to see what they can find out about her.*

You shouldn't do that, son. You need to get your information from her. He told her about the man and what Josh had told him. *Ah, well that is different. Yes, that's a good idea. The man should have been caught a long time ago for doing this to someone like her. But you tell her, when she wakes up, that we're here for her.*

I'm just going to test the waters here first. This is a lot to toss at her. She's alive, a tiger, and we're here for her. Mom, I'm not sure if you're aware of this or not, but we're too much for each other sometimes. A stranger that is hurting like Mason is could pull out a gun and shoot us all. Mom laughed, just as he'd hoped she would. *I'm going to contact Lily and let her know what I'm doing. If you could tell the rest of them, I would appreciate it very much.*

After talking to his mom, he felt better. Reaching out to take Mason's hand into his, he wasn't surprised to find it warm, her pulse running as his did, just a little high. Adrian decided that in the morning he'd bring his work here—not all of it, but enough that he could find himself some help. His dad had been begging him for weeks to let him be a part of his campaign.

When Mason opened her eyes and stared at him for a full minute, Adrian knew that he was in deep trouble. She was just like the other women in his life.

~*~

"What the royal fuck am I doing here? That man, the one that was on the bridge with me. He saved my life, didn't he? Why the hell would he do something like that? I didn't want him to touch me." Mason started to toss off her blankets when he stood up. They both stared at the damage that had been done to her in the water. "What happened to me?"

Her voice was low, and she could feel fear racing over her body. Fear of the unknown, as well as the little bits of things that flittered through her mind. A cat, tiger. Water in her throat. Hitting her head on something. Her broken arm and leg.

She didn't know who this person was, but had a feeling

that he was a Whitfield. It didn't make her situation any better, but she wasn't sure what to think about at the moment. Her body, it was a fucking mess.

"You had broken your arm and leg when he went into the water to get you. The scratches, those are more than likely from my brother and my dad. They saved you." She didn't stop looking at the long scratches, claw marks, that were running down her body. Mason asked him what they were. "Tiger, if that's what you mean."

"Yes. A tiger pulled me from the water." She looked at him then. He was most assuredly a Whitfield. "I didn't want to be saved. Do you have any idea what I had to do in order to do it before my father arrived?"

"Yes. I have an idea why you did it as well. I'll tell you why in a moment, but there are other things that I have to tell you first. I don't think you're going to like that any better than being saved." Mason leaned her head back on the bed and closed her eyes. The covers moved, and she knew that the man had covered her up. "You're a tiger as well."

"I see. So, not only did someone think that I was too fucking stupid to decide on my own life, they made me into an entirely different species so that I'd have a harder time doing it the next time." The man growled low, and she hit him in the face with her fist. "Don't pull any of your macho shit on me, buster. I had a perfectly good plan laid out, and your family fucked it up for me."

"I'm not going to tell you that I'm sorry. You should know that there's more. Much more that you're going to have to hear sooner rather than later. Would you like to hear it?" She drew back her fist again, and noticed that his nose was bleeding. He took her fist into his hand and put it on the bed, where he held it. "Please don't hit me again. I'm trying my best not to overwhelm you."

"You are, just so you know. What else is there? And start with the shit I have some control over first." He thought about it—Mason could see him mulling it over. Smiling, he told her his name. "I don't have any control over your name, fuck head. What is the matter with you? Don't you have any idea what is racing through my head right now?"

"Yes. I do. You're my mate." That was the final straw, and she ordered him out. But before he could get out the door, if he was even headed that way, her dad and brother walked in. "I've been waiting for them to show up. I have some things to tell all of you. As Mason suggested, I'm going to start with the things that she has control over first."

She'd not suggested anything, but demanded. When she looked at her legs, now covered by the sheet, she could see blood seeping through. And when her dad hugged her—tightly, like he was never going to let go—a small part of her was happy that someone had saved her life. Hugging him even felt better than it had before, she realized.

"Oh, honey, you're so lucky to have been found when you were." She looked at Adrian, then back at her dad, not sure what he knew or not. "If Oliver hadn't come up on you after you slipped and broke your leg and arm, you might well have frozen to death."

No one had told him, or Angus, if the look on his face was any indication. She realized she was still holding onto Adrian's hand, and shook free of it. Mason heard him laugh, but didn't comment. There was more to this than she knew about. And for now, she thought it better if she didn't speak.

"I'd like to talk to you all, if you don't mind. There are things that we need to talk about before you go home. There were circumstances that happened that day that made it so that Mason had to be—"

"No." She looked at her dad when she cut off Adrian. "Dad, I never...I lied to you. And I think this family was covering for me. I don't know why they did what they did, and right now, I'm—"

"Mason is my mate." Her dad hugged Adrian, then Angus hugged her. Her dad told her that he was so happy for her, and that she couldn't have done better than to be in the Whitfield family. Mason glared at Adrian, and told him to sit his ass down and to shut up. His laughter this time made her madder. But she turned to her dad and brother.

"I didn't slip and fall like they told you I did. I tried to kill myself." Her dad reacted just as she'd thought he would, denying that she'd do that. "I did, Dad. I went to the bridge to leap off it and to drown. Mr. Whitfield, Oliver, he did save me, but not like you were told. He pulled me from the water and then changed me into a tiger. He did it to save my life a second time. I was dying—as I had been before I jumped. I have AIDS, Dad. I got it from that guy Troy."

"I don't understand." She waited for Dad to ask questions, ones that she had too, but waited on him to come to terms, just as she was trying to do. "You said that you needed time away. You never mentioned that.... Well, I guess you'd not tell me that part, would you? What were you thinking? Okay, I know, you were thinking of saving me from—from your suffering, I guess. But you treated me unfairly, Mason. To have tried to end your life without even talking to me. I just don't know what to say."

He left her there. And soon after he left, Angus stood up and kissed her on the cheek. "I'll talk to him. But you should have thought this through, Mason. We love you very much."

Mason looked at Adrian when it was just the two of them

in the room. He didn't say anything, not even to tell her she should have let him handle it. Now she wished that she had. He might well have told them easier than she had. Or, more than likely, he'd not have told them at all.

"They're going to hate me now." Adrian said that he didn't think they would. "But you don't know. I should have just told him what was wrong before I tried to jump. What would you have done? I'm guessing that you're going to say something like, I was an idiot. Or that I should have been nicer than to blurt it out. Well, I don't work that way, and you'll have to learn to live with it."

"Are you finished?" She glared at him harder. "I told you that I had things to tell you. One of them is that you no longer have AIDS. You were cured of that the moment that you took your first breath as a tiger."

"It's incurable." He said that it wasn't, for tigers. "But it was in my body. What...does your father have it now? Will he die because he took it from me?"

"No, he's a tiger too. And as such, we're immune to such things like that. May I tell you more now that you seemed to have calmed down?" She nodded, not sure how much more she could take, but knowing she'd have to hear it sooner or later. "My sister-in-law, you'll meet her later, is a fae, and she gave you a little of her blood too, to help you along in the process. We haven't any idea what it might do to you, but all we really cared about—and I'm sure that your father will agree when he thinks about it—is that you're alive and well."

"Stop." He nodded and didn't say anything more. "I don't know what to say. I've been dealing with this, all of this, since I heard from the doctor all those weeks ago."

"I understand." She looked at him, and realized that he might well understand what she was going through. "I'm running for the senate. I've been campaigning for some time now, and my mom pointed out to me that I need to have help. So, I've decided to ask for it."

"I ran my dad's campaign when he was running for one of the local offices." He asked her if she'd like to help him. "We're mates. Aren't you going to order me to do it?"

"No. I'd never order you to do anything that you'd not want to." He smiled at her, and it was charming and soft. "I have a feeling that I'd be picking up my head across the room if I even tried."

"You'd be correct."

Laying her head back on the bed, she asked him things as they popped into her head, why she had the scratches being first and foremost. He answered her honestly, and then told her that he could never lie to her, even if he thought it was for her own good.

Chapter 3

Adrian sat down next to Mas. A glance in the corner made him see that they weren't going to be alone in this conversation, but for now, he was okay to have a seat. Adrian had spoken to his dad before leaving the hospital, to tell him that he was going to talk to the older man. Dad said that the last time he'd seen him was at the bar and grill in town, and that Mas had told him that he wasn't going to talk to anyone just yet.

"Can I answer any questions for you?" Mas told him to go away. "I'm afraid that I can't do that, Mas. You and I are related now, and I don't want you to be upset with Mason. She's feeling bad for not telling you."

"How did you find out? Did she tell you?" He told him what had happened, not even skipping over the part where she'd been changed into a tiger. "I could have helped her, Adrian. She's my daughter, and she was going to end her life rather than to talk to me about it."

"I think, in her mind, she was trying to save you and Angus from the pain that her suffering would bring you."

Mas huffed. "If it makes any difference to you, I think what she did was very brave."

"To have ended her life? What sort of bravery can that have been?" He told him everything that his dad had told him, as well as what Evan and Josh had said. And what she'd said to his dad before she jumped. "I wish I could have known. I don't know what I might have done, but she should have come to me."

"I don't mean to be rude, Mas, but what is it you would have been able to do for her? Nothing. She had to know that you'd do everything within your power to save her life. It wouldn't have done you any good. You'd still have had to watch her suffer and die." Mas ordered another drink, the first one still sitting untouched in front of him. "Why don't you and your family move into my house? It's large and—"

"You just want her there for yourself." Even after he said it, Adrian could see that he regretted it. "I'm sorry, Adrian. I know better than that, but I have to be able to lash out at someone. I think you can take it. But we won't be living with you. Not yet, at any rate."

"I was going to say that you and your family can live in my home. I have a place where I can stay. My mom would love to have me home to help out with Christmas and decorating." Mas said that he'd forgotten about the holiday. "Yes, so did I in all the hustle and bustle of what I'm doing."

"Your grandda, he told me that you had your eye on a bigger prize than being governor of the state. He's about to bust, he's so proud of you boys, as he calls you." Mas looked him up and down. "I guess he'd better take a second look at you *boys*. You're no more a boy than I am a woman."

They laughed, and Adrian ordered a platter of food. It wasn't the best way to start out a relationship with his new family, sitting in a bar, but it was better than Mas having him shot. As they sat there, waiting on their food to share, Adrian told him what he'd told Mason.

"Immortal? I guess that's because of the blood the fae gave her." Adrian told him it was from Tanner, the vampire. "You sure do get around, don't you, young man? Next thing you'll be telling me is that you know the president first hand, and that he comes around to help you with your campaign."

"He does." The platter was set in front of them both, and Mas laughed. "He's here now. As soon as he heard that I'd found my mate, he came to see me. Would you like to meet him?"

"No. Yes." Mas laughed. "You're not shitting an old man, are you, Adrian? I mean, if he were around, you'd think that someone would have mentioned it."

Henry sat down in the chair on the other side of Mas. He didn't say a word, but reached over and took one of the beers that was sitting in front of Mas. He just stared at him as he drank the entire bottle down in one drink.

"You don't get that kind of beer at the White House. You might want to remember that when you're there, Adrian. Hello, Mr. Barnhart. Your daughter is in good hands with this one. And she'll be a great deal of help when Adrian here gets to take over my job." Henry took one of the hot wings on the platter and asked Ben, the bartender, and the man who'd brewed the beer he was drinking, if he could have a towel.

"You're him." Henry started to put out his hand, but it was covered in sauce. "I don't mean to be rude, but aren't you supposed to be running the world?"

"Just this part of it for the moment. And I'm doing my job. I'm making sure that the next man in my position is just as trustworthy and honest as I am. And that the things that the two of us put into motion will stay there. For our future. As I said, Mr. Barnhart, he's a good man, and your daughter will be the best thing that ever happened to him." Mas looked at him before reaching for a wing himself. "Adrian, why don't you order us another round of these things and come to the table with us? I think we have some serious things to talk over."

They sat at the table as far from the front as they could. Ben knew who Henry was because he was working for him. He kept an eye on Adrian as well as the rest of the family, and reported back to Henry. It must have been Ben that told Henry what was going on. Dylan joined them a few minutes later and asked if they could take this to Adrian's house. She had some things to discuss as well.

"I've taken Mason to your house, and her brother is there with her. So is your dad, Adrian." Adrian asked how that was going. "Just what you're thinking. Your dad is falling all over himself trying to tell her how sorry he is for doing what he did. And she's getting angrier by the second. I thought I'd leave before blood was spilt and I'd be blamed for it."

When she had the cook in the back make up a couple hundred wings and said she'd send someone for them, he knew that this was going to be a long night and his family was going to be there. On the way to his house, Dylan told him about the things that she'd been able to find out about the man that had hurt Mason. None of it what she wanted to know, but they were working it down.

Dylan was good at her job, and if she told him that she knew a way to get to the moon without a rocket ship, he'd believe her. She was that good. She knew things that no one else might know, and was good at keeping them out of the newspaper. Sunny was like that as well.

When they got to the house, he could see that at some point, Mason must have convinced his dad that she wasn't mad at him. The wounds on her legs were healed up, and she wasn't nearly as bruised as she had been before he'd left her. The casts were for show, but she seemed to be getting around that all right too. The simple fact that she'd forgiven Oliver, without any reason to, made her wounds heal. It was odd that it happened that way. Adrian wondered if it had anything to do with the fact that at one time his dad had been the leap leader.

He sat down next to her on the couch. Adrian was happy now that he'd gotten furniture for this room, and for the dining room. The wings were set up in there, along with pizzas, tins of pasta dishes, and pies. There was enough food for an army, he thought, and hoped there was enough for everyone that was supposed to come by.

"I've offered you my home while you're trying to get things fixed up in the hotel." Mason asked him where he was going to sleep. "My parents still have our rooms the way we left them for the most part. I'm thinking that I could sleep in my lonely bed for a while."

After she smacked him on the shoulder, he got up to get her some food. Mason told him that she liked hot wings hot, and he decided to give her the volcano ones. He'd only had to eat one of them to know that they were much too hot for him. As soon as he handed her the plate with things on it for him as well, Dylan stood up and started talking.

"Mr. Barnhart, you've been wholly checked out. It wasn't just you joining our family, but if we're going to help with things, then I needed to know of all the skeletons in your closet and how they got there." He asked her what happened if he didn't check out. "We'll just leave that one alone, if you don't mind. There isn't any sense in muddying the water. But I think you might be aware of a couple of things that we found, and if you'd like, I can have them taken care of in no time." He asked her what they were. "For one thing, Mabel Clark. I'm sure that you're aware that you're not the father of Angus, and you should never have paid her in the first place."

"Yes, I'm aware of that. And I also saw the way that she treated him when I didn't pay her. I'm all right with her being around, I guess." Dylan told him that she was dangerous. "No, I think you're wrong there. She's greedy and a bitch, but not harmful."

"If you'd like to talk about it later, then I'm all right with that too. And then there is the company of White and Hall that wishes to buy you out. It's not the company that is trying to buy you out, but the son. He and his partner, a man that I think is smarter than the son, who has mortgaged everything he owns to do so. The money would be nice, but I don't think that's tempting you to sell, it is?" Mas only shook his head. "I didn't think so. It's nice to know that some people can't be bought. As a family, we've decided to help you out with this."

"What makes you think that I'd let you buy me out when I wouldn't let anyone else, young lady?" Mas looked at Sunny when she stood up. "My father started this business, and his father before him worked there. My children will have it when I'm ready to retire. Nothing you can say will make me change my mind. No, this is not going to go well if you try and push me into it."

"Perhaps it would serve you well if you'd not leap head first into making accusations that your ass can't cover, sir. Those men have bought all the land surrounding you, and have put in a proposal to have two high rises put in on all that land, including yours. They'll get approval, too, from what

I've been able to find out, and you won't have any choice in whether or not you wish to sell, you'll be taken anyway. And for not nearly what you should be getting for it." He asked Sunny how she could know that. "You might say that I have an inside track on such things. I'm fae, and I have a great deal of magic that lets me see things that others can't. And in this, Mr. Barnhart, you will lose."

Evan stood up then. "There are just over a thousand acres that we own as a family just outside of town here. It's already zoned for business, and it has water, electric, as well as gas on the land that we had laid some years ago." Adrian watched Mas; the struggle was hard on the older man. "We'll set you up on it, and make sure you have enough money to build and to expand when you want."

"What's this going to cost me?" Evan looked at him and Adrian stood up. "You own it, and you're going to blackmail me into something I don't want, aren't you? And here I was just starting to like you. Damn it—"

Aunt Bea came in the room with a plate of food. She politely handed it to him and then smacked Mas in the face. Mas held his hand over the place, but he didn't hit back. If he tried, he'd be dead before he touched their aunt. And Adrian only had to look around the room to see which one of them was going to kill him before he had a chance.

"Now you listen here, you idiot. And yes, that's what you are if you keep snipping and snapping at people when they're trying to help you out. My grandnephews are good men, and only want the best for good people. And here you sit acting as if they're going to steal pennies from a dead man's pockets. You sit right there and listen to what they have to say to you. When you have a question and not an accusation, then you can talk. Otherwise, you just keep that trap of yours shut. Understand me?" Mas nodded. "Good. Don't make me have to take you to the woodshed. I might strike you as an old woman, but I have no qualms whatsoever of turning you inside out should you need it."

Aunt Bea sat down, taking her plate of wings with her. Adrian noticed that she had the volcano ones, and he had to hold on to his laughter. Aunt Bea didn't say another word, and the room was silent. It wasn't until Mas cleared his throat that she looked at him again, but when he spoke, Adrian could hear the change of attitude right away. It would have been funny if not for the fact there wasn't a person in the room, Mas included, that didn't believe Aunt Bea would do just what she said she would.

"I'm sorry." Aunt Bea huffed, but Mas didn't look in her direction. "I've had a very stressful day, and it's taking me some time to get my bearings straight."

"It was only a bad moment, not a bad day. You can't think that just because things didn't turn out the way you thought they should on a single thing, that it's a ruination of a whole day. Just step back from it, regroup, and go on. That's what I do." Grandda sat down beside Mason, and took her hand into his as he continued. "You sure are a pretty thing, aren't you? Are you ready to have some kiddies for me?"

The room groaned, and Mas laughed. "I have been sort of in an odd mood. And I do apologize for it. But this thing with White and Hall, how certain are you that it'll go through?"

For an answer, Sunny handed him some paperwork. As he went over it, Adrian looked over at Henry. He was, for the most part, a family member too, and the investments that he had made for him over the months would bring him closer to them all when he was finished in the White House. He, too, was hoping that Mas would take him up on this offer.

It would hopefully bring more jobs to the state, as well as make Mas and his family a great deal more money than being forced out would do for him.

"This land, what else do you have planned for it? The reason I'm asking is, we've been talking about expanding into different areas of what we do now. As it is, we order all our produce for the wallpaper designs that we get. Angus said that he thought that we could run our own mill as well."

While they went over the paperwork with Evan and Josh, Henry came to him. "You'll have to talk to him about this Mabel person—you know that, don't you? It won't harm you any, not at all, but I think that it will go a long way in making sure that Angus is safe, along with Mas. He's a good man." Adrian told him he thought so as well. "Let Dylan find out what she can. And this other thing, with your mate—she told me that she can find him, no problem. Now that will help you."

"I don't care if it helps me out or ruins me. I want to find this bastard and make him pay for what he's done to her. Even if she wasn't my mate, I swear to you, I'd want him to pay." Henry winked, but it wasn't at him. Adrian turned to find Mason standing behind him. Pulling her into his embrace, he held her as he spoke to her. "He does have to pay, you know. There is no reason that he should be up and walking around hurting innocent people."

"I don't even know where to start." He said that he had a way of finding out. "All I know for sure is his first name, and that might not even be right. When the police went back to where I was being held, the place was on fire. There wasn't even a piece of tape left that he tied me up with."

"I can find him." They all looked at Josh when he came to stand with them. "I'm getting much better at researching things, and I'd like to help you. If you'd allow it."

~*~

Mason let Evan cut her cast away. It was scary, having a large electric saw so close to her leg, but she didn't jump or tell him to stop. And when he had it cut, it only took him a moment to tear it from her leg. She didn't even have a bruise or a cut on herself.

"You still have some deeper cuts on you. Those will heal if you will allow Adrian to be your mate. I'm not saying that's the only reason you should do it, but that is one of the perks." She asked Evan what another perk might be. "You'll be loved like no one else ever loved you. Cared for, pampered in a way that will make you wonder why you ever put up a fuss. Additionally, you won't have to worry about him stepping out on you, leaving you, nor will he ever lie or hit you. Never. Adrian won't be able to hurt you physically or mentally—not that I think he ever would, but those are just a few of the things that you'll have."

"I don't love him." Evan said it mattered little, that Adrian loved her. "That's not possible. We've only known each other a short time. No one falls in love that fast."

"We do. I guess it's part of our DNA to love fast and hard. Procreate as well. But even if it wasn't something that is inside of us, we do love with all our hearts." Evan put the saw away. "You should talk to the women of this family. They'll tell you whatever you wish to know. But be warned that they'll not hold back, and will just tell you like they see it."

"I'm not one to beat around the bush either." He nodded, and she stayed on the table where he'd been working. "Did you know that he's not even living at his home? I don't think he's at his mom's as he told me, but at a hotel. Don't you think that's sort of stupid of him? I mean, we could rob him blind, and there would be nothing he could do about it."

"No, but then he wouldn't care." Mason wasn't sure what to say to that. "Did you know that he put the house in your name? As well as the cars that you and your brother have been using?"

"No. Again, why would he do that?" Evan said she'd have to ask him. "I'm asking you, damn it. Why did he do that?"

"I think it was because you have no trust in him." She didn't so much as blink at him. Mason didn't trust anyone much anymore. But, she only just realized, she was beginning to trust this family. "Yes, I can see by the look on your face that he was correct. You should also know that he owns the land that he's putting up for your dad to use. All of it. He didn't want you to think that he was trying to buy you off to stay with him. We agreed to help him."

"I don't know what to say." Evan told her that wasn't why he'd told her. "Then why? Obviously he didn't want me to know. Or is it that he told you to tell me so that I'd feel something for him?"

"You have a very suspicious mind, don't you? No, he didn't do that at all. I told you because I wanted you to see him for what he is." She asked him what that might be, and Mason was sure that she knew the answer already. "He's a good man that has a good head on his shoulders. And a man that you could and should trust with your life. Adrian has been keeping things from you, things that he's terrified that will upset you, so that he can keep you safe. But, and this is from Dylan, the shit is going to hit the fan, and you should be aware of how much he's doing for you in the background."

"Such as?" Evan told her about the plans that he had for being president. "Yes, he told me that. And so did Henry when he was here. What is he doing for me to ensure that he gets the nomination?"

"When it comes to you, Mason, I don't think what he's doing would matter to him being president or not. He wants you happy. And in doing so, he's also keeping you safe. Right now, he's trying to find out, in small ways, if you'd rather he didn't take the White House and the position on." She started to tell Evan he was wrong when she remembered the few conversations that she and Adrian had had lately. "I can see that you've figured it out."

"Adrian doesn't think I'll want to be there. He's going to give up on this, isn't he? Because of me." He told her that it wasn't because of her, but for her. "There isn't a difference in that. He's still giving up his dream."

"To him there is a difference. He wants you happy. And in order to do that, he's willing to give up on something that he's thought he could achieve. But for you, he'd do anything." She asked him where he was. "Right now? I think he's in his office. Last time I spoke to him, this morning, he was working on some contracts for the state on a couple of fundraisers."

Picking up her coat, she turned and looked at Evan. "I'm sorry." He asked her for what. "For doubting you and the rest of your family. But if I have to murder him over this, I do hope you'll remember me fondly. Because if he gives this up, or even thinks about it anymore, I'm going to beat him to death with my shoe." She felt embarrassed. "I've been hanging out with your grandda too much."

Evan was still laughing as she left the building to get in her car. Adrian had been responsible for this too—a means for her to get around. And the only reason she knew about it was that the dealership had called her to find out what color she'd wanted. But she hadn't known of the title being in her name.

She was at his office in no time, but sat in the parking lot for a few minutes. Pulling her cell to her, she called Dylan and, lucky for her, the other women were with her. It was time to make a stand. Not against Adrian, but to find out what she could about Troy and what he'd done to her.

"I need your help," Mason said as soon as Dylan answered the phone. "I want to find this bastard, and I need to know how to keep Adrian on the right track to be president. I think he'd do a wonderful job at it."

"Then you know that he's talking to Henry about quitting." She said that she'd not known it had gone that far. "I'd go see him first. He was at his office when I spoke to him earlier. Well, spoke is a loose term. I might have knocked him around a bit. And if you really want him to do what you want, then I'd ask to have him show you how to shift. Of course, there will be lots of sex involved. Are you ready for that?"

"Honestly? I have no idea. I've been brutalized, and I haven't any idea how I will react. That's some of why I've been avoiding him." Dylan said for her to tell him that. "Look, I don't need help with my sex life, just what to do in finding Troy, or whatever his name is. Can you do that for me?"

"Oh yeah, we can. But we'd like to be near you and Adrian, or at least you, when we do. You see, we can find all the men if we put our minds to it. It would be helpful if we can narrow it down to him." She asked why they couldn't find them all. "I like you. A great deal. Yes, we'll work on it, but one of them at a time, ending with Troy. I want to be there when he pisses himself when you find him."

After setting up a time to go and see them, Mason got out of the car. She was stopped no less than a dozen times by people thanking her for helping with the job situation. She wondered what they were talking about until she remembered her dad had been going to look at the new site. He must have taken them up on the deal. Good for him, she thought.

Then there were a few that congratulated her on finding Adrian, and told her what a nice man he was. All the more determined to give him a piece of her mind, Mason stomped toward his office and right past Lily, who worked for Adrian.

"What the fuck do you think you're doing?" Lily didn't even bother leaving them, but said that she'd been asking him the same thing. "You think that it would serve anyone if you no longer want to run for president?"

Lily laughed hard and loudly. "Oh, Adrian, I like this one. She'll do you a world of good at the White House." Lily reached for the door that Mason had slammed to the wall when she'd opened it. "You guys have a nice talk. Or whatever. I have to get home so that I can— Well, I do have to get home. You two have fun. And Mason? Welcome to the family."

Mason thanked her, and told her that it was yet to be decided if she wanted to be in this idiot's family. Crossing her arms over her chest, she looked at him again.

"You didn't answer me." He leaned back in his chair and she moved closer to it. "Why are you deciding, without talking to me, to give up the presidency? I've only known you for a little while, but you don't strike me as a quitter."

"I don't think I can run it and be there for you. You didn't even act like you wanted anything to do with what I've been doing." She swiped her hand over his desk, clearing it of anything that was there, including a large stack of papers. "You do know that I'm going to have to put this all back in order, don't you? I mean, I have obligations to the state, and you just tossed it aside."

"Well, you should be used to that then, tossing things

aside." That had sounded better in her head. "You are not taking this job because of me. Do you have any idea how that makes me feel? How much you're going to hate me when this opportunity passes you by?"

"No. I'd rather have you as a mate and happy then to run the free world." Mason climbed up on his desk, crawling toward him across the expanse of it. In that moment, she knew that she not only wanted this man in her life, but that he was already in her heart. "What do you think you're doing, Mason? If you're trying to make a point, I don't understand. All I can think of is how much you remind me of a cat. Which you are one, by the way. We should—"

"Shut up, Adrian." His teeth came together so hard that she heard them. "I'm afraid of sex. I mean, I had it before Troy, but not since. I'm terrified that I won't be able to enjoy it. I don't even know if I could make you enjoy it."

"Do you want to make love with me?" She nodded, and sat down with her legs on either side of his chair arms. "You're making it very difficult for me to think. And if you— Holy Christ, woman."

She dug her toes into his cock. He rocked upward into her, and she pushed him back down in the seat. Mason was watching his face, making sure that he wasn't repulsed by what she was doing. By the look of pain on his face, she still wasn't sure.

"I am serious, Adrian. I don't know if I can do this." He told her that if she kept that up, he'd surely show her how she was making him feel. "Is that enough for now for you? For you to enjoy this even if I can't?"

She never saw him move. One second, he was sitting down on the chair, the next he had her pinned to the desk. But he was careful of her, not making any moves without telling her what he was going to be doing. Reaching up to his face, Mason cradled it in her hands and pulled him down for a kiss. His body, all of him, was all she could think of in that moment.

"I want you, Mason. I want to make you scream out my name. To be able to touch a part of you that only I can. Do you have any idea how much I've wanted you since I first saw you?" She moaned out his name. "We're the only ones in this building, love, and I'm going to make you scream in pleasure so much that you'll be hoarse from it. I love you, Mason Jane Barnhart. And I'm going to prove it to you until you're faint from it. And me too."

When he touched her clit through her jeans, she screamed. It was the first real orgasm that she'd ever had, Mason realized. Sure, she'd enjoyed sex before, but nothing like this. And when he stripped her of her clothing, just a loud tearing of her things, she laid there before him like a feast. A feast that she thought she was going to enjoy feeding him.

Chapter 4

Adrian wanted to hurry, but his beast, this time, was slowing him down, telling him that they had the rest of their lives. That she was theirs and no one else's. Even as he suckled her nipples, feasted on her entire breast, he was careful not to rush her, waiting for her to show him some sign that she wasn't afraid of him. That was the last thing that Adrian wanted.

"Your skin feels like silk. I'd like nothing more than to drape you in the material for the rest of your life. And diamonds." He kissed her navel, where she had a piercing. "You'll have to remove this, I'm afraid. If you shift with it there, your tiger will be hurt."

"Take it out for me, Adrian." He wasn't sure how to do that, but did put his mouth over the small piece of jewelry. It simply fell apart in his mouth. "Yes, that's wonderful. Please, I need more."

He cupped his tongue in the small indentation, tasting her blood as he healed the small wound. And when he had enough of her there for the moment, he kissed her hips, her pelvis, then made his way up her rib cage one rib at a time.

"Mason, put your arms up over your head. I need for you to not distract me while I explore you. And I'm seeing that I have a great deal to explore, too." She said that she wanted to do the same to him. "Men have nothing like a woman to look at. You have these lovely breasts that tighten when you're aroused. The perfume of your skin when you're dewy like you are now. The way your breaths speed up, the smell of your breath on my skin—all things that I want to know about you. And your pussy. Christ, the smell of you, the smell of your neediness, is almost too much for me."

"I need you. Please, don't tease me anymore."

He leaned to her pussy after making love to her breasts, neck, and throat. He loved the way she tasted everywhere. And the more aroused she became, the more her scent made him want more of her. Licking her from gate to clit, then nipping at the wonderfully responsive nubbin, he grinned when Mason screamed out her release.

Adrian drank from her greedily. She tasted of what he thought heaven would be like. Her nectar was thick and hot—the more that slipped from her womanhood, the more he wanted of her. But he had to have her. Now.

Standing up after taking another deep drink of her, Adrian entered her slowly. Filling her was both painful and beautiful. He wanted to take her slowly, fill her with himself so that she'd know it was him and only him that wanted her, that loved her. The way her body responded to his had him breathing hard, holding onto his release as best he could so that she would come first.

"Adrian, now—please, now."

It was all it took to take him completely over the edge. He pounded her hard through two more releases as he let go once, then again deep inside of her. Taking her up and off the desk, he slammed her against the wall, taking her harder there as he ravaged her mouth.

"I love you, Mason. I'll love you forever."

She kissed him then as he came again, his body spent. Adrian knew that his heart was going too fast—his head felt light—but when she took his throat, biting him hard enough that he saw stars, he came again and again until her screams stopped.

"I love you too." He looked at her. Adrian wanted to believe her, wanted to feel like it wasn't just the aftermath of fantastic sex. "I do love you. Stop looking at me like a speck on your sweater."

"Okay, first of all, I don't wear sweaters. They're too hot for me." He kissed her and staggered to the couch, holding her to his body. "Secondly, I can barely breathe, much less think that you said that so I'd take you again. Which, by the way, will kill me if I do."

She giggled, and he held her closer to him. "No, I think you broke me too. That wasn't anything like I thought it would be." He asked her if it was better or worse. "Christ, Adrian, I don't think in all my life I've ever come that many times. Not to mention, that hard. What are you, super fuck man?"

"Yes. That's my nickname. Super Fuck Man." Turning her in his arms so that she was sitting across his lap, her legs on the couch, Adrian looked at the paperwork that was a mess all over the floor. "You are going to help me fix those papers. Not that I care that you did it—and you are more than welcome to do that again to me—but next time, let us be slightly more careful with paperwork."

"All right. The next time I come to your office to seduce you, I'll take the time to remove all the things from your desk first." He told her never mind. That would take too long. "Exactly. Now that you've had your way with me, is there something you need to tell me?"

"Yes, I nearly forgot." He got up and went to his pants. They were in terrible shape, but he knew that he'd hang them in his closet for all times. Getting the ring out of his pocket, he got down on one knee to propose to her. "Mason, will you be—?"

"That's not what I meant." He told her to hush. "No, I won't hush. What do you think you're doing? You can't just ask me to marry you while we're both naked."

"Why not?" She said she didn't know. "Then Mason Barnhart, will you be my wife? My first lady, even if we never make it to the White House? Will you love me? Have children with me? You do want children, don't you?"

"I do. Finish up, please. I want to kiss you again." Adrian told her that she messed him up. "Then yes, I will marry you. And we'll have tons of children, and have a lovely time in the White House where, I want you to know, I plan to shake things up a bit. I will forever love you until the end of time."

"Good enough for me." He slipped the ring on her finger. "I love you. And because I have to have a nice big wedding, I'm going to have to insist that your father let us pay for it."

"Why?" He told her what Henry had said to him. "Ah, I see. Dignitaries and stuffy people. You can ask him, but I bet you that he'll turn you down. He's like that, you see."

"I know. That's why I was hoping that you'd help me." Adrian got up and found his duffel in his closet. After taking out a pair of jogging pants and a T-shirt, he handed them to her. "Would you like to go home now, have a nice dinner, and run in the woods with me? Tomorrow will be hectic enough, after announcing to the world that we're going to be wed."

"Sure. And if you are nice to me tonight and make me come a few more times, I'll be standing right beside you when you announce at our engagement get together that you're going to be running for president. By the way, this ring is beautiful. Where on earth did you get it?"

"Grandda. He used to buy my grandma jewelry all the time, especially when he was in trouble. Which, I'm to understand, was a great deal more than any of us thought." They were both laughing as Mason pulled on a shirt of his, as well as the sweats. "We'll put things in there for you from now on."

They sat on the floor and straightened out his paperwork. Mason would read some of the papers, then stack them up. He was glad when she had opinions on things, and was thrilled when she offered him advice on a couple of his key points.

"You want to bring more businesses to the state, I'd start with companies that have been sending things overseas to be worked on or finished up. My dad, I guess he's taking you up on the land, right?" Adrian said that he was. "Good. And he's going to build the mill too. You could say that. Tell people what Dad is doing here, and that would make people realize what an opportunity it would be to bring their businesses back home."

"We can't announce that your father is coming here until he's been made another offer on his business. And once he accepts this offer, he and my brother are going to the board of directors of the firm of White and Hall and telling them what an underhanded thing their front men are doing; or in this case, the owner's son. I guess they were doing this without their permission." She asked if that was serious. "Not to us, no. But it does mean that the purchases they've made so far could be considered null and void. If that happens, then we swoop in, buy up the property, and put in a business rather than a high rise. While that is something that we can use here in Ohio, it's not a priority. Jobs are."

"What happens when all these people are employed again?" Adrian asked her what she meant. "Well, the schools will be overwhelmed, won't they, with new hires coming to the area? Also, there will be more pressure put on day cares, as well as people who just babysit. That scares me more than anything about this. The number of people babysitting from their homes that aren't bonded or checked to see if they should be doing it would be very high, I would imagine. I'm not saying that all home sitting places are bad, but there are quite a few that are."

Adrian sat back, thinking about just one of the things Mason had mentioned and the potential issues that it could cause. As he sat there thinking, she got up to get paper from the drawers of his desk and started a list.

"What do you think we can do?" Mason asked if he had a laptop she could use. "No. Use the one in the desk. I had just put it away before you came to see me. Not that I'm complaining, mind you. But by doing that, I might well have saved its life."

"Good thinking. I'll need one too, if you want me to help out on this thing. That is, if you don't mind. I think I could have some input. Not all of it will be good stuff, but something for us to think about." He told her that he wanted her to help out on everything he did. "If you don't, will you promise to tell me?"

"Yes. But I can't think of any time when your input won't be something that I value." He watched her type in the search bar. "What are you looking up?"

"Grants and other monies that we can use for free for

schools to upgrade and make improvements where needed. Even if they just need some upgrades, there has to be money out there for it." He showed her his list that Henry had given him a few days ago. "This is perfect, Adrian. There is a great deal of things that we can have worked up with this list."

They worked for nearly three hours. When he felt his belly rebelling at being empty, they ordered pizza and subs. By the time they were finishing up for the evening, he'd ordered her and himself new laptops, knowing that they'd have to be hooked up to secure networks, and had several applications for funding on hold. Now all they had to do was get the other end of the project going.

~*~

Mabel waited on hold for nearly ten minutes before the person at the other end came back to her. Andi, as she'd said her name was, was going to be on her list of shit to get from Mas when she finally got in touch with him. This bullshit of having to go through this person was for the birds.

"I'm sorry, Ms. Clark, I can't transfer your call to him. I'm afraid that you're going to have to leave a message after all." Mabel told the bitch that she was beyond leaving a message for Mas. "Then I don't know what to tell you. He's out of touch with the company right now, and told me that he'd contact me when he was ready to take calls or messages."

"So you talked to him." She said that she had, he was her boss. "Give me the number that you have for him and I'll forget this entire thing. He owes me money, and I am not going to be put off like some sort of bill collector."

"I don't believe Mr. Barnhart has ever had a bill collector calling him. But if you don't want to leave him a message, then I guess there is nothing more than I can do for you." There was a hardness to her voice, one that told Mabel that she knew just what she wanted Mas for. "If there is nothing else, then I have work to do."

"You hang up on me, and I swear to Christ you'll regret it." The woman laughed, like Mabel was teasing her or something. "Get him on the fucking phone. Right fucking now."

"Nope."

Then the line went dead. The mother fucking bitch had hung up on her. As gently as she could, Mabel hung up the phone. Then when rage took her over, she picked the handle up and beat it against the pay phone until it broke.

It had taken her two days to find a pay phone. She'd gotten her a phone with the last cash he'd given her, and now that she was broke again, the service had been shut off. Getting Mas to pay monthly for her to have one was out of the question, he'd told her. Mas was going to do it this time, or she'd take her kid back.

Mabel didn't have any idea how old Angus was. She knew that he had to still be a teenager, or close to it. When she went to collect money from Mas, she never saw him. She supposed that was his doing too—keeping her from seeing how good looking and grown up the kid was. Besides, when she was high, or drunk, whichever she had the money for, things sort of just floated away, not clouding her memory at all.

Mabel didn't know who his father was, but had found Mas's name in the newspaper and was happy at how profitable he'd been. But it was time to up the game, she thought as she walked back to her home, which she could use but not sell, and that she had gotten from her dealings with her sugar daddy.

Mas had purchased it and put things in it for her to use, but she couldn't sell any of it. Once a month, on random dates, someone would come by and inspect the place. One thing missing and she'd be out on her ass. Again.

"Fucking bastard never did trust me." She laughed at that. She'd not have trusted her either. But it was galling that he held all the cards and she had shit.

Mabel pulled in the newspaper that came every day, and tossed it to the pile that she'd sell off later to the scouts or something. But before walking away, she noticed his name on the first line.

Pulling it to her, she saw that Mas's name was attached to someone else's. And his daughter was getting married. Mabel supposed at one time she'd known he had another kid, but not much more than that. Reading the entire article, she nearly wet herself when she turned the page and saw the house that the couple would be living in.

"Christ almighty. I hopped on the wrong pony with this one." The man, Adrian Whitfield, was the governor of the state of Ohio. That narrowed down her search, she thought. Mas would be at the wedding for his darling daughter.

Now all she had to do was get from here to Ohio as soon as possible. Things were going to be fine now, she thought. Mas would not want her to fuck up the wedding plans of his little girl. Mabel might even get herself an invite to the big event. Surely for the mother of his little boy, he'd see his way clear to do that.

"And if he doesn't, then I'll have to crash it. And I do mean crash it." She thought of being able to topple the wedding cake, watching it tumble to the ground. Maybe she'd get in the house and tear into the wedding party and ruin the wedding dress. As she thought and planned, the level of trouble she was going to cause grew bigger and bigger.

The only way she knew to get money was to fuck for it.

But Mabel knew that being on the up slide toward fifty-five, not many would want her. It was a sad time, she thought, when a woman couldn't make a living on her back no matter her age. And Mabel thought she still had a lot going for her, too.

Going to the liquor store, she waited in line, still thinking of what she was going to do to get there. Her bottle of wine was the cheapest shit that she could pull out of the fridge, but it would give her a nice buzz since she was desperate.

Just as she got to the counter, she saw that the manager had a heavy bank bag in his hands. She watched as he carried it under his coat to the soft drink area. That was just what she needed, some money for her to take. And by the looks of it, there was a great deal to be had too.

Going back to where he was, she commented on how cold it had gotten lately. He didn't speak, but made a grunting sound. Looking around, she knew that they were alone, and took her cheap shit and hit him in the head. Then for good measure, she banged him four times while he was down.

No one came after her. So, looking around again, she reached up under his coat and took the bank bag from his limp hand. It was heavier than she'd thought it would be, and realized that it had a lock on it. Since Mabel didn't want to fuck around in the store much longer, she simply put down the bottle she used and made her way to the front of the store. To be caught stealing the cheap shit now would land her ass in jail.

She was nearly sick with worry that they'd catch her. Not that she would go to jail—no, Mabel was too slippery for that shit. The counter guy, a man that she'd blown for some of the better wines they carried, waved at her and she waved back, just to make herself look normal.

Out the door before she could get caught up in something that she didn't want to deal with, she was racing to her home about the time she realized that she'd left her prints behind. Then she remembered that they didn't have her prints. Not one time since she'd been in jail had anyone asked for them. Or at least she was reasonably sure they hadn't.

Not even bothering to go home, she went to the first nice restaurant she saw. Of course, the fucker was closed up, so she had to settle for all night burgers with so many onions on them they made her slightly sick. But the food was hot, and so was the coffee.

Taking the bag to the bathroom, she was glad to find out that it was a single shitter and that she could lock the door. Cutting into the canvas bag, she nipped her hand and got blood on some of the bills. By the time she had wrapped up her hand, there was someone pounding on the door.

"Damn it to fuck, I'm taking a dump. Will you go the fuck away?"

The man said he was only looking for a place to sleep, and she didn't bother telling him that she was there again.

Dumping out the money, she nearly did shit herself when she saw the bundles of money that she had. Eleven thousand dollars. Holy shit, she thought, he must have been holding onto the deposits all day. Counting it again, she was thrilled to death that she was going to be able to go to Ohio, but she had to be careful too.

Mabel didn't like being careful with money. It was meant to be spent, have fun with. But after she made it to Ohio, she told herself, she'd be able to have as much fun as she wanted. The fucking dick was going to pay for putting her off so much.

Putting the cash in different parts of her clothing, she was just getting ready to leave the bathroom when she thought about her hand. It was bleeding pretty good now, and she watched in fascination as the blood dripped into the sink.

Wrapping it in the hand dryer paper, she threw all the bundle wrappers in the trash. Then for good measure, she put more papers on the top of it to hide that she'd been in there with it. As much as she was bleeding, she did worry about DNA or some shit. But again, she didn't think that anyone would have any of that shit either. And if they did, they'd taken it without her permission, and they'd not be able to use it against her.

Mabel had to stop herself from skipping. Mas was in for some serious payback when she got to him, and his daughter too. Mother fuck, she might even have to raise her son for a bit once they were both dead, as he'd get all the fucking money.

Going home, she packed what she would need. She decided that since she wasn't all that good of a driver, she'd just take the bus to him. Mabel didn't think it would be all that hard. Just sit on her ass until they arrived. She even had the name of the town that the wedding was going to take place in.

It was cheaper than she thought it would be—just about forty bucks for a one-way ticket. It wasn't like she would have to come back on the thing. She'd have enough money for a jet, she realized, when this was finished.

The next bus was to leave in two hours, so Mabel made her way to the coffee shop to drink the hours away. But as she was going to the little coffee place, she noticed that there was a little shop. Who didn't need a little something new when they were traveling? she thought.

She ended up spending two hundred dollars. After finding a bag that she simply had to have, she noticed that they had wine too. Buying the largest bottle she could find, she also bought herself a large thermos. Since she couldn't pull out the bottle and drink from it, she simply filled the thermos up and smiled to herself at how clever she was. Sitting in the coffee place now, she distributed all her money and new things to her bag and ordered not just a coffee, but a Danish for now and one for later.

"You're going to pay me or die. And dying would help me so much more than you living, I think." She looked around to see if anyone could hear her. When she noticed that she was alone except for an old man, she laughed again. "Yes sir, Mas, you're going to pay with your life if I have anything to do with it."

Chapter 5

"He said yes, Mac." Allen White was thrilled beyond words to hear those three little words. He asked his partner in crime, David Ward, to repeat them. "I called Mas Barnhart yesterday, and then again this morning when he was out of the office. He called me back today and I flat out told him, sell or it's going to be over for him. He said he'd sell."

"You really threatened him? Good for you. Ballsy, but good. The money we'll be making off of this will show my father I'm not just a bump on a log. He'll have to respect me now." David sat down in Mac's comfy chair. "When are we going to meet up with him? Did he give you a time and date?"

"He said that he'd be able to come back home for a few days at the beginning of next week. Since it's Friday now, I'm assuming he means that'll be Monday." Allen mentally rubbed his hands together. "I got a call from The Brewery yesterday too. They wanted to know how soon they're going to be getting their money. The guy told me that they're nearly moved out."

"He's never getting it; you know that, right? Idiots should

learn to read the fine print on contracts."

That had been a stroke of genius on his part, he thought. The last few lines on the second page said that if there wasn't any check accompanying the contract when it was signed by both parties, then the amount would be void but the land would revert to Allen White.

"Christ, I should have been in charge of this place long ago. Can you imagine what sort of income we'd all be having if I was? And when the company that is building the high rise comes through with their money, we'll be sitting at the big boy table, David, mark my words. There isn't any way that Dad is going to say a thing to us, what with the income we're generating on this one deal."

"You still think that he'll make me a partner in this? I mean, I've worked just as hard as you have, Allen. I don't want to be left behind, buddy." He asked him if he'd ever lied to him before. "Well, yes you have. A great deal, as a matter of fact. That's why I keep harping on you about this deal. I seriously don't want this to be only feathers in your cap."

"I will not leave you behind, David. There, does that make you feel better?" When he didn't say anything, Allen turned back to the bar that was in his office. It was only ten in the morning, but this was cause for celebration. Asking David if he wanted one, the man turned him down. As Allen thought he would. "This will make millions—hell, billions—when this is all said and done. Christ, you having that idea about getting a cut in the rentals was brilliant. That will make Dad take notice of you if nothing else does."

"Yes, well, this firm that I rent from, they told me that I'm paying the rental group a fee each month to be able to—"

"Yes, yes. You've told me this before. As soon as you hear from Barnhart again, I want to know. And the sooner you have this meeting with him set up, then you make sure that I can be there. This is going to be epic. I cannot wait to rub it in Mason's face that I'm the one that got poor Daddy's business." Allen danced around the room. "She will have to marry me now, don't you think? I mean, damn it, I do hold all the cards."

"She could still turn you down, you know. Mason made it pretty clear that she didn't like you. I think her words were she'd 'rather be eating worms and drinking piss than to even be in the same room with you.'" Allen felt his temper rise up and sort of slap him in the face. Of all the things to bring up, Mason belittling him in front of a group of his friends had been the last straw. "What if she still turns you down, Allen? Have you thought of that?"

"She won't. Not when she sees that I'm the one holding all the cards to her dad's business." He wasn't, not really. He was going to take it from him, as he had the rest of the people's businesses around him, and sell it to a conglomerate for even more cash. "And if she does, I don't really care. Mason will be with me or else. I'm sick of her turning her nose up at me."

Big Al, as everyone called his father, walked into his office without knocking again. When he simply eyed his watch, then the drink in his hand, Allen put it on the table and walked away. He wasn't afraid of his father, but he didn't like him either. He was a bully and an arrogant ass.

"David? Am I just paying you to sit around sucking up air? I don't think so. Get to your own computer and get to work." David shot out of the room so quickly that the door didn't even close all the way before he was sitting at his desk. "Allen, what is this I hear about you making waves in the business world?"

"What do you mean?" His heart started pounding, and he

had to sit down or fall over. "Maybe you can be more specific. I have my hand in a lot of things."

"I'm not talking about your hand up some woman's ass, shit head. I'm talking about asking for a loan from the bank. You do know that I have told them they're not to lend you a single dime, don't you? Until you pay me back what you owe, then all funds are cut off from you. And since I don't foresee you ever paying me back the twenty-six thousand that you owe me, I guess you should be living from check to check about now."

"I don't know how you expect me to get things done if I can't even take a client out to lunch." His father told him that was for him to do, not his low life son. "Why is it you call me names all the fucking time? What did I ever do to you?"

"Let me start with the most recent." Dad even pulled out a notebook, like he was keeping track of it all. "Three days ago you wrecked a car that wasn't yours to even be driving. In fact, I don't believe you've had your license returned since the last few times you fucked up. The dealership, in the event you didn't know, is pressing charges for the money for not just the two-hundred thousand dollar car you wrecked, but also the display window that you drove it out of. Then there is the party that you threw at the IBEW hall, without permission from the group. There was not only nearly fifty grand in damage there, but you managed to get into their safe and take the cash they had there as well."

"It was my birthday, and since you didn't have a bash for me, I decided to throw my own." His father pointed out that he was thirty-one years old. "So? I noticed that you had a bash for your sixtieth birthday."

"Because that's a milestone, you moron. Although I can see where you'd want to celebrate being the ripe age of thirty-one. Who would have imagined that you'd make it to twenty, much less eleven years longer?" Allen asked him why he hated him so much. "I don't hate you, Mac. I just don't have any feelings for you whatsoever. I did, a long time ago when you were young enough to stay out of trouble. Now? Well, now all you do is cause me grief and cost me money. More money than any man should have to pay for a child of your age. When are you going to learn the value of money?"

"I know what things cost. I just don't have the funds to buy them. Oh, wait. That's your fault too. Even my paychecks are less than anyone else's. Why is that?" Dad told him that they showed up to work on time and put in forty hours of working time. "I'm here that much."

"Yes, and don't think I didn't notice that you left out working. You think I don't notice that you come in late every day, and that you leave earlier than most people do? That you take two and three hour lunches, and sometimes don't come back after leaving at eleven?" Allen wisely said nothing. What could he say, really? It was all true. "When you grow up, which I don't foresee happening anytime while I'm alive to see it, I'll give you more lead way. But, like I said, I don't see that happening."

His father sat down at his desk and looked like he might be staying there for a while. Allen couldn't help it. He sat there staring at him for as long as he could without speaking, all the while feeling like his insides were going to burst.

"What the hell are you doing now?" Big Al just laughed at him, as he did whenever he thought he had the upper hand on something. Pissed off that he had so little regard for him, Allen blurted the first thing that popped into his head. "You'll be surprised to know that I have a plan in the works that is going to make us millionaires."

"How much is it going to cost me?" That's all he had to say about his plan? No questions? Christ, Allen thought as he stood up, he really hated his father right now. "Do you mean the plans for you to take over my job someday? It's not going to happen, Mac. You're not going to take something that I've worked so hard for and run it into the ground in a week."

"You haven't any confidence in me, do you?" He said that he didn't. "Why? Other than me being a man having fun, why would you treat me this way? When all I've wanted to do was be your partner here?"

"You never wanted to be my partner. You only wanted what the money could do for you, and you know it." Allen sat back down in the chair; his father didn't trust him with anything. He'd known it, he supposed, but now it was right out there. "At your age I had a wife and you. I knew in order to sustain my family and myself that I had to work hard and make sure that they had a roof over their heads as well as food in their belly. You spend my money like it's water, and there is an endless supply of it."

"You never wanted to have fun. And look at what it did for Mom."

Allen would swear, if asked, that his father had leapt over the desk and pulled him up out of the chair by his neck. He couldn't breathe, much less speak.

"You ever say a bad thing about your mother again and I will rip your throat out where you stand. Do you understand me?" He nodded. Then when he was dropped, Allen fell to the floor, his legs weak with the power of the grip his father had had on him. "In less than a month I'm selling my company. I'm sure that the new owners will not keep you on the way that I have. All the locks will be changed, and you'll lose what things you get as perks from here. I would suggest that you figure out something else. I'm finished with you as of this moment."

Allen got up, holding onto the chair next to him while he coughed around his painful throat. When he was seated, he looked around the office and decided that there wasn't any point in being here. Not ever again. As there was nothing of his in this place, he couldn't find a thing in here that he could sneak out that security wouldn't take from him.

Going out to David's desk, he told him what his father had said to him, including the sale of the business. Of course, instead of asking him if he was all right, David was more focused on losing his job. Allen told him that he was leaving and that he was coming with him.

"No, I don't think so." Allen asked him why not. "Two reasons. As I stated before, I don't have a great deal of trust in you. I only went into this because I didn't think you'd follow through. Secondly...well, that sort of goes back to the first thing. You aren't going to be able to pull this off, and I'll not only be out of a job, but more than likely in jail. You're simply not a closer, Allen. You never have been either."

"You think you're going to get arrested?" He said no. He thought that they both would. "You're as bad as my father. Just looking out for yourself."

"Perhaps you should do the same thing, Allen. I mean, if he did that to you, what do you think he's going to do to you when he finds out that you went behind his back with this, and that you used his good name to cheat a great many people out of millions of dollars?" David looked at his desk before continuing. "No. I might be a fool, but I don't think you're going to be able to do anything like you said. And I've been thinking about it—I don't think your father is wrong about you. You are a lazy fop. And you're a drunk, as well as an ass. I'm staying right here until I can't any longer."

"Are you shitting me right now?" David handed him a note and told him that it was Mas's number. "You mother fucking cock sucker. When I own this building, the first thing I'm going to do is fire you."

"Yes, well, if you ever own anything that your dad didn't give you, I'll let you hit me too. But if you look deep enough, you'll realize it was a pipe dream in taking down Mas Barnhart."

Leaving the building, throwing his keys as well as his badge to the guards, Allen was happy to see that he hit one of them. As he made his way out to the parking garage, two things occurred to him. His apartment key as well as his car key was on the keyring. And he was going to have to go back in there after his grand gesture to get them back.

"Mother fuck, will nothing go my way?"

Storming to the door to get his things, he found the guard he'd hit with his things just standing there, his arms crossed over his more than likely drugged up massive chest, and shaking his head at him.

"This means war; you know that, don't you?"

The guard just laughed. Allen was going to get all of them. And as he made his way to the street, something else occurred to him. He didn't have any money for a taxi.

~*~

Adrian needed to talk to Mas. And in order to do so, he wanted back up. The man had been nothing but wonderful to him, from the moment he found out that he was going to be his son-in-law, to this morning, when Adrian had come over to have breakfast with Mason's family.

"I have a question for you. It's about the wedding plans." Adrian had nodded, not bringing up again that he'd pay for it. That hadn't gone as smoothly as he'd hoped. "I've been thinking that while I do have a great deal of money, giving my lovely daughter the kind of wedding that I think she deserves will cost me the world."

"All right. She's been trying to cut corners for the cost. Were you aware of that?" Mas said that she'd come to him last night with a second-hand wedding dress picture. "I don't have a problem with her doing that, and you shouldn't either. I'm sure that you taught her the meaning of a buck, just as my parents have all of us."

"Yes, but my little girl is going to marry a man that could very well be president of the United States soon. I want her to shine." Adrian said to him that she did shine. "You're a sap."

They both laughed. And when Angus joined them a few minutes later, they talked about the wedding and how quickly it was coming up. As they parted ways that morning, Mas had thanked him again for helping him out with the wedding. And now he had to talk to him again about something.

Just as he entered the living room, Adrian was almost weak with relief to see Evan there. Not only him, but his dad and grandda as well. When he had a seat with them, he realized that Mason had had the room decorated. He'd have to check out the rest of the house. He'd been stuck in his office all day.

"There you are." He hugged his family. Dad continued with whatever they'd been talking about before he entered. "We were talking about the wedding coming up, and the venue that your mom is fixing to use. I tell you, Adrian, this is going to rival your getting to be president bash."

"Dad, he's not even announced it yet. Why don't we wait and talk to him about it first?" Adrian asked his dad what about it. "Well, Dylan and the rest of them think you should announce at your wedding day. That way, everyone will be in a good mood and you can feel good about it too."

"I don't know. That might take away from the day for us, don't you think? I mean, something like that, I think we need to run it by Mason." She walked in the room and sat on his lap, asking what they were going to run by her. "Dad and Grandda think we should announce at the wedding that I'm putting my bid in for president."

"What a perfect idea." He asked about it taking from the wedding. "Oh, pish posh. We're inviting all those dignitaries here for the soul purpose of buttering their wallets up for your campaign. Why not tell them now so they can save up? I think it would be wonderful to give them something to think about rather than what we might be doing on our honeymoon." Everyone laughed, and he had to admit, it had its merits.

"Pish posh?" Mason grinned at him, and he hated to take away her good mood right now. But he had to let them all know to be extra careful. "I've found out some news. None of it good, I'm afraid."

"She's coming here, isn't she? I don't think we have to worry too much about her. I know I said it before, but Mabel is stupid, not dangerous." He handed him the police report, as well as the picture of her killing the manager of the Stop n' Go. "Oh dear God. She killed this man? Why, do you know?"

"Money. She'd been in line at the counter when she must have seen something that led her to believe that he had cash on him. And a great deal of it too. Eleven grand. Mabel followed him to the back of the place, looked around, and then bludgeoned him to death with a large cheap bottle of wine. She didn't even bother with taking the bottle with her when she left, leaving behind fingerprints and DNA. Before leaving, Mabel took the bank deposit from him. The police have an all-points bulletin out looking for her, but so far nothing. This happened yesterday in Chicago."

"That poor man. I see that she did it, but I just can't believe it. Was there anyone there? I mean, witnesses? Did she hurt anyone else?" Adrian looked at Evan. "Please tell me that this one man is the only one she killed. One is bad enough, but any more than that, and I just...I don't know what to say."

Evan picked up the tale with what he knew. "She's killed twice now that we're aware of. Dylan has an eye on unsolved murders now. And when she can, she's cracking into surveillance cameras to see what she can find out. This morning, she called the police to tell them that she'd seen a dead body at the car dealership. There were two people there that Mabel murdered." He asked Evan if she'd robbed them too. "No, this was over a new car. They wouldn't let her 'borrow' it for a few weeks and she'd pay them money. I guess Dylan said it looks like the owner laughed in her face. She pulled out a steak knife and killed him. Then, while rummaging through his desk, she found a gun and killed his wife that was there dusting the cars for the day. Mabel took the car anyway, and lucky for us, it has a LoJack on it. Dylan and the rest of them are tracking her every move."

"I'm not doubting you, not at all now. But what would she be coming here for? I mean, she has money now."

No one knew, but Mason asked how she'd found out where they were. This time Dylan answered as she came into the room. She then handed them each a single sheet of paper to read. Adrian put his on the coffee table, knowing what it said already.

"That wasn't as easy to figure out, I'm afraid. She called your office, apparently, and asked for you. She was told then that you were out of town and they didn't know when you were to return. Which was what your office was supposed to tell them. However, your announcement was put in the papers, and we can only assume since Adrian's the governor it was picked up by papers all over the world. She knows not only that you're in Ohio, but that you are all here."

"Christ, this is terrible. You tell me what I have to do and I'll do it. I don't care what it costs me to have this woman out of my life for good." Dylan asked if he was in a hurry to have her gone. "I'm not sure what you're asking me."

"We need to do this one thing at a time. The meeting for the sale of your business should be done first. I've learned over the years that doing the easy first makes the hard stuff seem less overwhelming. One thing at a time and we'll get through this." Mas asked Dylan what happened if she showed up too soon. "You don't have to worry about that. I have people causing her little hiccups along the way. She'll be at least another four or five days over what it would normally take. And if I have to, I'll have her arrested before she can arrive. I have connections all over the world, I'm sure you've come to realize."

"Yes. I'm beginning also to see that you're not one to mess with. And I won't, not unless necessary. About this meeting—I don't want you to think that I doubt you, because as surely as I'm sitting here, I won't anymore. But you're sure that I'm not going to lose my business?" She grinned at him, and Mas looked at Adrian. "I don't think that's very reassuring, do you? I mean, does she look at you like that sometimes?"

"She does, but I know that whatever she is planning will be precise and epic." He laughed with Mas and the rest of them. "I'll be with you on this too. I have a law degree, and as much as I wanted to look over the contracts that they're having others sign, I missed one very important item in yours.

In it, it says that if the seller doesn't receive money when the contract is signed by both parties, then the money contract is null and void, but he'll still own their business. It's buried well, but I feel bad that I didn't catch it. Before I forget, the attorney for Henry is going to be there as well. He said that we're to follow his lead on this. And for us all to wear casual clothing."

"I'm assuming there is a reason for that, but all I can think about is Mabel. Angus, he never liked her, so I don't know how this will affect him." Adrian told Mas that he'd told him earlier, as he'd been in the room when Dylan made the discovery of the dealership people. "I'll have to go and talk to him. I don't want him to feel that this will make any difference to me."

"He knows that. Angus was more worried about how it was going to make you feel." Mas said that he really didn't know. "I'd still go and speak to him, but he looked to me like he was taking it very well."

After everyone left and Mas went to talk to Angus, Mason sat on the couch with him and told him that she had a few things that she wanted to run by him. He said he was hers forever if she needed him.

"First, let me say that your mom is scary organized. And a little…I was going to say rude, but that's not it." He told her she was persuasive. "Yes, she is that all right. The invitations are going out today. She told that printer that if he didn't do this for her, she'd kick him out of the readers' club. That must be a big deal around here, huh?"

"Yes. There are a few groups that my mother is in, and she gets things done. What else did she do? I'm assuming that she got you to do something for her." Mason said that she hadn't done anything, but she was asking her all the time what she wanted. "Did you tell her what you wanted?"

"She already gave me what I wanted. You." Adrian kissed her. Knowing that it could and would lead to more, he pulled away to let her finish. "Also, I want to work out something that will have both your dad and mine giving me away. I don't know how we can make that work, but I need to work on it. Also, and this is a biggy—I think you should ask Henry to be your best man."

"I don't know. It's that thing again, with taking away from our wedding." She shook her head and smiled at him. "You've been hanging out with Dylan and Sunny too much, my dear. What do you have up your sleeve?"

"If you announce, and I really think that's a good idea, then what better way to get people to take notice than to have a president standing beside you when you do?" He asked her if she'd given this a great deal of thought. "Yes. While I was trying my best to be excited about wedding dresses and who is going to be my bridesmaids—which I have figured out, but am not telling your mom. She'll have something to say about it, I'm sure."

"You mean she'll not think you chose well?" Mason said it wasn't that. "Then what, honey? My mom can be very persuasive, as we've said, but she's not going to tell you no on your wedding day."

"I want her to be my maid of honor." Well, Adrian thought, that would be something his mom would have something to say about. "See? Anyway, bridesmaids are Dylan, Sunny—who I just love. I love Dylan as well, but she's scary—Carter and her sister Rachel, plus Ivy. For some reason she said that I needed six, so I have to come up with one more. Know anyone? Because I was thinking of asking Lily to help me out."

"She'd have a rooster." Mason cocked a brow at him. "I'm not even going to apologize for hanging around my grandda. I love him to pieces, and he always makes me laugh. And I know for a fact that you play chess with him. And checkers."

"He cheats." Adrian burst out laughing. Everyone knew that his Grandda cheated at chess. It was the only thing about him that made Adrian not want to play with him. "And you know what? He's not all that good at it either. But I don't say anything. I think he enjoys thinking that he's pulled a fast one on me."

"Dad cheats too, by the way. I think he learned how from Grandda." She nodded and leaned back on the couch. "You look exhausted. Am I wearing you out?"

"Yes. But this would be so much better if you lived here, and I didn't have to feel like some morning I'm going to find money on the dresser." Adrian told her that he'd never do that. "No, but it would be nice to wake up with you. All this sneaking around because of the press is annoying as fuck."

"We found the first man." That made both of them sit up when Carter came in the room with them. "He's going to be taken care of today."

"Do I want to know?" Carter just smiled and shook her head at Mason. "Okay. I don't then. And you have all their names now? I mean, the thread or whatever it's called, you know each of them?"

"Oh yeah. We know all nine of them." Adrian hadn't realized it was nine men. "Troy Foster is going to be shitting his pants soon enough. Especially when we get to number six on the list of soon to be dead men. That's when he'll realize what might be going on. That's not necessarily the order we're going to take them out, but he was the sixth shit hole that we found. That guy is his longtime lover."

Chapter 6

Mason was sitting in the library, not really doing much but watching the snow pile up around the deck. She couldn't wait until summer, when she could enjoy the pool and the deck around the entire house. As she was getting ready to go and refill her tea mug, Carter came in to sit down.

"I'm sorry if I'm interrupting you. And I hope you don't mind, but I had your butler, Andrew—nice man, by the way—bring us in some refreshments. He said you missed lunch." Mason asked her what was going on. "I'm building up to it. Are you all right?"

"I don't know. I have this mad woman after my brother and father. A group of men that raped me over days and days and gave me something that would kill me. I tried to kill myself over it, and was saved by a tiger who changed me into one, by the way. Also, Christmas is in a couple of days, I haven't the slightest idea what to get anyone, and I'm getting married on the fifth of January." Carter laughed. "I might have left out a few things, but I think you understand."

The tea trolley was brought in, and it was filled with

sweets and a large urn of tea. There were lemon slices too, as well as lumps of sugar to go in the tea. After taking another cup of tea and a scone, Mason asked Carter what was going on.

"You know what I can do, right?" She nodded. "Well, I sort of kinda got into the police station, where they were holding your clothing. I touched your shirt that was still in lock up. You should be aware that these men, they have done this before and after you. Of the five women that are still alive of the ten, not counting you, two more are very near death. I'm sorry."

"I am as well." She looked at the tree in the corner of the room. It was beautiful, and had a great many gifts under it. "I've been shopping online for gifts. I think I have everyone done. I know I said that I was at a loss, but I've done all right. I had the most fun with the new babies. There are a great many things that can be a learning tool for them. Of course, being the aunt, I didn't get them those. Nor clothes. I got noisy things and fun stuff. Tell me the rest, Carter, please?"

"Mabel has killed another person. I know you think we're letting this go on too long, but I assure you that we're not. Dylan said that as soon as she crosses the state line, she'll be arrested. And the more we can pile on her plate, the longer her jail term will be." Mason didn't say anything. She had been thinking that. "Josh and I can travel. Like, we can go to see someone without them knowing, and for some reason we can touch and move things. I've healed the person in the second convenient store. Also, I read Mabel's mind. She's broke, as you might well have guessed, and she's at the border and is planning to rob the bank there in a smallish town. Once she goes in and pulls her gun, she'll be finished."

"They going to kill her?" Carter said only if it came to

that. "I see. So, this person that you healed, why them? Why not the people that are suffering from Troy's evilness?"

"I can't do that. If I do, and they were set to die, then it happens anyway, at some other time, and usually more horrifically than they might have before. And as you know, dying the way they are is about as horrific as it gets, I think." Mason nodded. "The man that I saved, I've asked for permission from my mother, and she said that she could and would protect him. He has a wife, a new baby on the way, and he cares for his mother and father. I just couldn't let that happen to him."

"I understand. Do I know your mom?" Carter smiled, and Mason smiled with her. It was friendly, not like she had a fat secret that she wasn't sharing. "Why do I have the feeling that she's someone scary?"

"I'm not." The beautiful woman appeared in the room and Mason stood up, spilling tea and scone crumbs all down the front of her. "No need for that, child. I just wanted to make myself known to you, that's all. I'm Sennetta. I have no last name, but I usually go by my title. I'm the queen of the fae. My mother, Breen, recently retired, and is now having a good time here in this realm."

Mason looked at Carter, then back at Sennetta. They looked like sisters. The older woman had wings, however, and she wondered for a brief moment if Carter did as well. When she stood up and spread them out behind her, Mason had to sit down. It was too much.

"I might have to revise my list of things going on. I don't mean to be rude here, but could you please just put those away? They're beautiful, very much so, but I've had a hard time of late, and I'm only just getting my feet under me again." They both laughed. It sounded like wind blowing gently through a windchime. "You're here because you wanted me to believe? I'm not sure what this could prove, to be honest. I believe in a great many things that I hadn't before."

"No. I think that would be rude." They were both sitting on the couch now, and Sennetta seemed to be less sparkly. "I came here to ask if we may do you a favor. Well, all the Whitfields. Your wedding is coming up, and we should like to make you and Adrian shine. With magic. But no one else would know—they'd only see a beautiful couple in love. You would show that right now you are a very beautiful woman yourself, but this will make people more apt to...." She looked at Carter.

"Vote for him. Trust him more. It's not to make them vote for him, but it will show him in a better light. And that way when the time comes, he will do what he said that he would do. Plant more gardens for the faeries. Also, and my mom seems to think you being in the White House will help, there will be more children born." Mason told Carter that she didn't understand. "Fae love children. Their happiness, their laughter. Also, it gives the fae more energy, I guess you could call it. And when a child is born, all over the world, a fae is with them. At least until the time that they no longer believe in them. It's like Santa, I guess."

"I'll have to talk to Adrian, but I don't have a problem with it." Sennetta said that he'd said the same thing. "But he was busy today, and said he would ask you tonight. I'm pushy at times when I love someone as much as I do Adrian. He's like a son to me. But I should like to start now, if you would not mind."

"Go for it." The house trembled, and she had to close her eyes with the movement. "Holy nut crackers, that was some magic. What did you do?"

Then she looked at the tree. It had been decorated by the staff. Ornaments had to be bought for it and the other three trees. But this one in here with her, it seemed to move. And all of a sudden, a thousand little creatures moved around on it, and it changed in not just color, but the way it glowed.

"I don't know what to say. It's stunning." Carter laughed and told her that she should see hers and Josh's. Mason went to stand next to it, and that was when she noticed that there were more gifts under the tree. That the star on top that she'd not particularly liked was now a bride and groom. "This is gorgeous. I know that I keep saying that, but this is amazing."

"Your home is now protected more than the men in suits can do, as are the rest of the family's homes. Your family will be safe from all manner of creatures that are not welcome here. And you will know happiness for so long as you live." Mason thanked Sennetta. "Your father too—I have given him good health and longevity, along with your brother. Your father, Mason, has been ill for some time, though I don't think he knew it."

They talked for a bit more, this time just about the wedding. Sennetta asked if she had her dress yet, and Mason told her that they were still looking. Mason told her the problem. She was embarrassed.

"I know that it's silly, but Adrian and I want to have children—a lot of them—and I want a dress that my daughters would want to borrow. One that will be timeless in its beauty. A shining example of the love that I have for their dad." Her face heated up. "I was looking for a second-hand dress. Not because of the cost, like my dad thought, but the wedding dresses of yesteryear were so beautiful. They paled in comparison to the happiness that you could see on the bride's face, and that's what I want. A dress like that, but not. Am I making any sense?"

"You are and you have." Sennetta asked her to stand up. "I think I might be able to help you. Just give me a moment to see what you have looked at. Ah, I see that you have thoughts of different things from different dresses. This will be tricky. I'm going to have to ask you to go to the stairs for me, please."

Mason did as she asked and stood up on the fifth step in the long winding staircase. The room seemed to tighten for just a moment. Mason closed her eyes when told, and felt her clothing change. Into what, she wasn't sure yet, but when Mason was told to open them, she looked down at herself.

The dress was white, as pure as the snow that was falling down outside. The sleeves were long and simply lace, beaded flowers of what looked like diamonds interspersed on them. The neckline was high, and it too was covered in the same little beads. The dress itself was slim—not form fitting, but flaring out ever so slightly at the hips and trailing behind her on the floor. But it was the veil that caught her attention, a long trail of lace and bead work that she thought would be heavy, but didn't pull at the tiara where it was attached. And when Sennetta said a word in a different language, the faeries, she knew now, from the tree graced her dress all around the lacy edge, giving it the appearance of being flowers in the spring.

"I don't know what to say. It's perfect. And the veil. It's...I don't know what to say, but thank you. So very much." Andrew came into the hallway and dropped the tray he had in his hands. He stared at her like he couldn't believe it. "What do you think, Andrew?"

"My lady. I have never seen a more beautiful bride in my entire life. You are magnificent. Lovely, and oh my, so very beautiful." He didn't bother to even pick up the tray when he walked to her train. "What a nice addition to such beauty, my lady. The faeries have given you such color."

"Is this what you wanted, Mason?" Nodding around the tears, she told her that it was just what she'd wanted without knowing it. "Good. Also, I will supply you with your flowers. You will love them as well. But alas, I must go. I have duties as the new queen that I cannot neglect any longer. Oh, before I forget. You now have the ability to shift your clothing. Just think of what you wish to wear and it will be there for you. As for the dress, after the wedding, it will be taken care of and cleaned by my staff, as it is magical. Then it will be brought back to you to store away for your own children."

Wearing jeans and an old T-shirt, she went to the woman and hugged her tightly. Mason didn't have a mother, and she'd grown so fond of Aunt Bea and Eve. Now this woman was a part of that group too. Women that she could look up to and admire.

"I cannot thank you enough for this. You have made something for me that I will treasure forever. And our friendship too." Mason hugged Sennetta. "You must come to the wedding. Please, I'd love for you to be there with us. But if you'd not mind, leave the wings where they are."

"I will be there. And my wings will stay just where they are, unless there is trouble. But I do not foresee anything that will ruin your day."

Mason hugged Carter then, and Carter left with her mother.

It had started out with bad news, but ended on a very high note. Just to test out the dressing thing, she thought of the wedding dress again. The faeries were there as well, and there seemed to be more of them. Mason loved it, and this was something she'd treasure forever.

~*~

Mabel moved into the bank and waited for her turn in line. She knew that there were cameras all around the place, but she didn't care. She had taken precautions on it, wearing a wig that she'd picked up at the Goodwill store and old men's clothing. Mable scratched at her head again, just knowing that she'd gotten something from the stupid thing.

Who knew that money could go so very fast? She had had a good time and a couple of parties, but it hadn't been that bad. Then just yesterday morning, she'd gotten up and realized that she only had two hundred dollars left. This time, she told herself, she was going to be much more careful.

Two more people shuffled in the line ahead of her. Mabel looked around. There seemed to be a lot of people here today. When she'd come in yesterday there had been about ten. But today it looked as if all the tellers were at their places, and the guard at the door seemed to be younger as well. Oh well, she wasn't going to rob the entire bank, just this one teller. She had the most people in her line.

"I can help whoever is next."

Thank goodness, Mabel thought, one of the people in front of her moved to the next line. One more person and she'd be ready to take the money and run. Christ, this was as easy as taking candy from a baby.

Mabel thought of all the gifts that were piled up in her car and trunk. She'd gotten her boy something for Christmas, and had gone a little overboard. But since she wasn't sure of his age—he was more than likely about seven or ten—she had gotten him things that she saw other women buying for their own kids at the mall.

Angus would come with her. She didn't really want him, but he'd come with her. She knew that she'd not treated him all that nicely as a little baby, but she'd not really wanted him.

But she was going to make him want her over Mas. Then, if that didn't work out in her favor, she would murder the old man, which would give him no place else to go but to her. Then Angus would inherit it all. Mabel wasn't worried about the girl. If she remembered right, she was sort of stupid anyway.

The Christmas tree to her right was huge—the thing had to be about ten feet tall. And there were gifts under it, probably empty boxes. But it looked good. Very festive. It made Mabel long for a tree of her own. However, she didn't want to mess with putting it up or taking it down. That was why she'd never had a tree in her life. They were just way too much work for the little bit of shine you got from them.

She was moving up to the cashier when she pulled out her note. Mabel didn't want to make a scene—she just wanted her money. As she handed her written note over to the girl, Mabel pulled out her gun and pointed it at her chest.

"Say a word or press any buttons and it will be the last thing you do." Mabel was very proud of herself—she'd practiced that several times over the last few hours. "Put all the money in that bag."

"Don't move." The man behind her, who had been waiting in line with the rest of them, spoke as he rammed something hard into her back. "Put the gun on the counter and no one will get hurt. Especially you."

Putting the gun on the counter as she was told to do, she turned around and looked at the man. But it was the room that had her staring. Every person in the place, from the old bag that had moved to the other line to the tellers behind the little holes, was pointing a gun at her.

"What the hell is this? I didn't do anything." He reached behind her and pulled the bag that she'd given the teller.

"That's not mine. I don't know what you're doing here, but I'm not going to jail."

"Mabel Ann Clark, you're under arrest for grand theft, the murder of Jon Dennison...." As he droned on about this and that, she watched as if it was business as usual. The clerks were all back at work, the guard at the door was now the old man that she'd seen yesterday. Looking at the person that was speaking, she put up her hand to shut him up.

"What the hell is going on here?" He said that he was arresting her. "For what? I mean, you guys entrapped me. That's it. You were here waiting for me, and that's not right. How did you find out that I was coming in here today? Because from where I am, it looks like you had someone tell you of my plans. I don't think that's right either. Let me go, and I'll try and forget this entire thing."

"Just like that? You think I should just let you go after you killed five people that we're aware of? Killed someone in the process of a robbery?" She asked him when she had done anything like that. "When you stole the car and killed the man and his wife while they were there."

"Oh yeah." She giggled. This man could not be serious. "You haven't any idea who I killed or when. So let me go right now before I get really pissed off."

"Go ahead, please. Because I have permission from my boss to blow your fucking head off if you so much as look like you're going to resist arrest." Mabel didn't believe that at all. She'd not done all that much. And it wasn't like she was robbing the entire bank of their money.

"Wait, you're arresting me, and I didn't do anything wrong in here." He just stared at her, like he didn't believe she was speaking. "Seriously. You don't have any right to hold me on anything, because I didn't rob this place. And I'm sure they would have padded that amount when they sent it into the insurance company, and you don't have any idea what I've done or not. Let me speak to your boss. Right now, jug head."

He put out his hand to the man standing on her right. He handed the gun toting asshole something. He showed her the first of what seemed to be pictures. The thing was in full color, and it showed the blood splatter all over the refrigerators beside her. It sort of turned her belly a little. It was someone beating the guy from the convenience store.

"That could be anyone." He showed her the next picture, one of her covered in blood, the body just inches from her as she looked right into the camera. "Still, that could be anyone."

He just growled at her and turned to the man standing next to her again. She didn't know either of them, nor the woman that was dressed in a skin tight black and camo outfit. Mabel wondered if she'd ever looked that slim and in shape. And when the first man backed out of her way, the woman stood in front of her.

"My name is Dylan Whitfield, special agent to the United States. And I'm his boss. What did you want to ask me? And just so you know, Mabel, I'm already looking for a reason to end your miserable life."

"What a way to talk to someone who has done nothing at all wrong." Dylan Whitefield, special agent to the United States, laughed at her. "What the fuck do you find so funny?"

"We have it on good authority that you're going to find Angus, and also murder Mas. That's not going to happen, but I do have a question for you. Do you know this man standing here?" She pointed to the man that had had the pictures. "Look at him closely and try to remember anything about him. His eye color. The way his hair is wavy. Anything you can use to tell me if you know him."

Mabel thought this was a stupid thing to ask her, but she did what she wanted. Whoever he was, the man surely was tall. There wasn't anything about him, nothing to make her believe that he was anyone that she knew. And when she turned back to look at Dylan, the man spoke.

"Hello, Mother." She looked back at the man. "Yes, I'm your son. Angus. And I'm so glad to know that you're finally going to be behind bars."

"No, you're not him. What sort of tricks are you playing on me? My son is a kid, and he's going to help me get all the money from Barnhart. Who are you?" He pulled out a couple more pictures, these of him in one of those different picture thingies. Then as she studied the pictures as he grew up, she looked back at Angus. "You'll help your old mom, won't you? I mean, it's about time we get to spend time together. Come on, tell them, Angus. Like you used to do in the old days, tell them I'm a good mom and should be left alone to do what I want."

"You were a horrible mom and a terrible person. You had me lie for you. You beat me and tied me to the floor. And when you'd run out of money, you'd clean me up, take me to Dad's house, and demand more. Why didn't you just get a job? No, I'm not going to vouch for you. For all I care, you can rot in hell, you fucking bitch."

And he just walked away from her. Mabel looked at Dylan and asked her what happened now. What did she have to do to get out of this? And would she please call Mas Barnhart so he could place bail.

"Are you kidding me right now? Christ, woman, you've been on a rampage for three days, and you would have gone on with your killing and robbing spree if we'd not stopped you. What did you think was going to happen when you were caught?" Mabel wasn't stupid, but she knew her rights and told Dylan that. "Your rights mean shit to me right now."

All she did was touch her. Just a simple brush of her hand against hers and Mabel screamed. It wasn't that there was any pain; no, it was the images that were coming to her, flash after flash of things she'd done to get ahead all her life. From being in gang bangs to doing some nice mellowing out drugs. The murder of the man in the library when she'd been ten. The bus driver that had refused to let her off at her friend's house when she'd been fourteen. All the way up until today. Then she saw what would have happened today, she supposed. The teller was killed, by her. The three men at the other counters were killed when the money that she'd gotten had exploded in blue before she'd left the place. The old guard didn't even get to draw his weapon before she shot him in the nuts, then the face. As she went running out of the bank, not a bit of money to her name, the cops were waiting for her, all lined up and yelling at her when she waved at them.

Bullets hit her body then. She was shaking from it; her entire chest and face were blown off her bones. And the blue on her hands from the canister going off mixed with her blood and became a pretty shade that she had no name for. Then it was all gone.

"Had enough?"

Dylan stepped back from her and Mabel wondered if she'd answered. Before she could form a response, or even ask her where she'd gotten that and how had she known about the events, she was in the back of a cruiser with her hands cuffed to the back of the seat in front of her. Mabel's ankles were also latched down, like she was going to get fucked from the rear. It was all too fast, she thought. None of this could be real.

Looking out the window as best she could, she saw Angus waving at her as she was driven by him.

Chapter 7

Troy looked out the window for anyone lurking around his place. Mathew was with him, but he was little to no help. The fucker jumped when the toaster pushed the bread up. He was like a cat in a room full of rockers.

"What's going on?" He wanted to tell Mathew that someone was out to get them, but he figured that he already knew that. Of their crew of nine, what they called themselves, there was just him, Mathew, and Sam left. Christ, and the way that they'd died. "Did you see Sims when his body was pulled out of that building? He looked like someone took a needle to him all over his body. And his dick? Why would someone do that to his dick, Troy?"

Sims—Simon Sanchez—had been with him for the last ten years. Ten years of blissful fun. He just knew it had something to do with the women. The way the rest of them had been mutilated had been hate and nothing more. And the police were doing nothing.

"I asked the cops what happened to him. You know what they said? That he'd committed suicide. I don't think anyone could have thought that after looking at him." Troy shivered. "Someone is coming for us, Mathew. And I'm scared shitless."

Neither of them had left the house in two days. Tomorrow was Christmas, and they didn't even have any bologna to share between them. Sam had gone out earlier this morning to get something for them to eat—anything, they'd told him—and now they were getting worried.

"We might have ordered a pizza if I wasn't scared that whoever is doing this would do to me what they did to Chuck. Christ." Troy nodded at Mathew, keeping an eye out. "What do you suppose they used on him?"

The phone call from him only said for them to come over, he had pizza, which Troy had thought was strange. Chuck didn't like pizza—hated it, even. But when they got to his apartment, there Chuck was laying with his feet hanging out of the doorway and blood everywhere. His face nearly looked like the everything pizza that was laying on the floor. And his dick, like the others, had not just been cut off this time, but was laying on the pizza, all cut up to look like some strange pepperoni. Troy vowed right then that he was never eating pizza again.

Allen and Ross had been in their home when they were killed. He'd not seen it—they were the first of them to be killed—but he'd heard that seasoned cops had been sick from the blood all over the walls Troy had heard that the words "I'm coming for you all" were left behind, written in their blood. "Have you seen or heard from Tommy lately? I heard that he was getting out of town on the first flight out. I wish I'd have gone with him now." Troy told him that he was dead too. "How'd he die?"

"He was dropped from an airplane. The police thought that he was trying to stow away and didn't get in the thing in time before they took off." But that wasn't all of it. He'd seen his body in the morgue before he'd been cremated. "They sure messed him up, Mathew. I don't think the fall did all that to him. And all his bones, they were broken into tiny pieces. My friend that works at Shidler Funeral Home, he said that the police had a hard time picking him up. He was like water, he was so broken. And they didn't find his dick either."

That sort of made him sick too. To think that someone was taking dicks, like they were something that you'd put on your mantel, or even the fucking Christmas tree.

Troy saw a car drive by slowly and his heart started to pound. But when it drove on, pulling into the driveway down the street, he relaxed a little.

"Where is Sam? I thought for sure that he'd be back by now. Christ, how long does it take to get some food?" Troy told Mathew that there were a lot of things on the list. "I guess so. But I'm about starved."

So was he, but not enough to go out and try to forage for anything. This was a nightmare. Troy thought about Richie, the last of them that had been killed. He wasn't even going to think the word, and cursed himself when he did.

Richie had been at the bar where he worked part time. Most people wouldn't hire anyone that had AIDS, but this bar sort of catered to their kind—the sick, lonely, and dying. There was even a jar on the counter that had money in it. Before it would be filled almost every night when they left. Now there was barely enough for them to use to buy a beer.

Another vehicle drove by, a truck this time. He didn't bother watching where it went; he knew that it belonged to the man down the way. Instead of thinking about how to get out of this, he thought of Richie and how he'd been...well, murdered seemed like such a tame word for what they'd done to him.

His mouth and eyes had been glued shut. Troy had thought it was to keep him quiet and not to see anything, but since they were going to kill him anyway, why glue his eyes? Not only had he had his dick removed, but he'd also had every one of his fingers and toes cut off. Then they were glued back on this body. Fingers where his toes should have been, his toes on his hand. And if that wasn't enough to sicken a person, his entire body was carved with the names of women. Women that Troy knew were the ones that they'd taken.

"Troy, did you hear that?" He hadn't, he was so deep in his fear of what was happening. The worst part was, he didn't have any idea who would be doing this to them. Not that they didn't deserve to die, but come on, what the fuck? "I think that Sam is back. He must be putting the bags on the stoop in the garage."

Before he could tell Mathew that he didn't have a stoop anywhere, he heard the door open to the garage and the screaming. It seemed to be endless and painful to his ears. Troy didn't want to go and see who it was, or even what was being done to them. Hiding out sounded pretty good to him, but he did go and he did see. There was Sam, his friend who had helped him come out. The man that had given him his first kiss. But it wasn't really him, his mind screamed. It was something. Something that he'd never be able to un-see for the rest of his life.

Like before, he'd been glued back together. His legs and arm were now in different places. His head wasn't on his body, Troy only just realized, but turned upside down near his shoulders. His belly was cut open, his guts on his head like curly fries. Christ, he thought, he was never going to eat again at this rate. Then he turned and threw up three times before he staggered back to the living room to await his own fate. In an abstract sort of way, Troy wondered what sort of person could do that. Then he remembered all the things he'd done to people.

Sitting in the chair, he watched as Mathew brought in two bags of something. When he went to the kitchen, Troy got up to find out what he was doing. He was going to get the rest he told him—they'd eat well tonight.

"So much food. Sam must have gotten a good deal on it. Look at this steak, Troy. I think the two of us could share it and not be hungry afterwards. There are baked potatoes and cereal. Not the kind I like, but that's fine." The refrigerator door opened and Mathew put in the milk and butter, then put in the eggs. Troy was sure that he'd lost his mind. "How about we have fettucine Alfredo? My mom used to make it all the time. She'd put chicken in it for me."

"Mathew? What's wrong?" He said that there wasn't anything wrong, but there was a kind of detachment in his eyes, like he'd checked out without paying the bill. "What's wrong with you? We have to call the police."

"Oh? Why, did something happen? I'm going to start on dinner. For some reason I'm about to starve to death. Oh look, Troy, here's an apple pie. I'll put it in now, and that way we can have it warm after dinner. Come on now, you go and set the table and I'll fix this up."

He did as he was told, going to his dining room to set the table. Troy wasn't completely sure what was going on with his friend, but if he wanted to have a nice meal after this, then by God, they'd have one. Pulling out his mother's old china set and her silverware, he set the table in style.

"Troy, I'm making me a cup of tea. Would you like some? Sam got the good stuff, and it sounds yummy." He said sure as he stood over the dinner set, trying to remember the order of the forks. "This is going to be so nice, don't you think? I might even have to spend the night, I'll be so full."

If he spoke anymore, Troy didn't hear him. The silverware was giving him fits. But after he gave up, he set not just the plates out with the matching glasses, but he also thought the bread plates would be lovely, as well as the pretty tea set that was with the set. When he had the table looking as good as he could, he decided they needed candles. It might take their mind off of things if they could just be normal, Troy thought. Normal? He wasn't even sure if that word had any meaning to him any longer.

Getting the candles from his room, he skipped over the last time they'd used them in this house. His birthday had been a few months ago, and they had celebrated in style. Looking for the lighter, he asked Mathew how much longer and didn't get an answer. Going into the kitchen, he slipped in something and stood up, laughing at his clumsiness.

His smile dried to his face like it had been glued there. His teeth dried out so much that he couldn't have closed his lips if he'd wanted. Mathew was there, standing in front of the sink—leaning, more like it—and he was surely dead. The amount of blood that was flowing from his neck and wrists was too much to think that he'd come back from this.

Troy looked at the floor. Mathew's footprints were smeared in the blood, like he'd cut himself and then walked around the kitchen to finish dinner. There was blood on the stove and the tea pot that had started to whistle. Troy wasn't sure what was more sickening, the fact that he'd done this without making a sound, or that the man had made his dinner for him.

Backing out of the kitchen, he moved across the room.

They were all dead—all his crew was dead, and had died horribly. Leaning against the wall that led to his bedroom, he could only stare as the blood from the kitchen started to move toward him, soaking up in the rug that his mom had put there to wipe his feet and not hurt the hardwood floors.

Sliding to the floor, he decided that he'd take Mathew's way out—just kill himself and be done with it. Crying now, not even realizing it, he staggered down the hall to the room that he and Sim had shared, and stopped when he saw the woman sitting on his bed.

"Oh no, Troy, you're not going to kill yourself, are you? I have plans for you." He asked her who she was. "That's not important. Suffice it to say that I have a vested interest in you being dead. By the way, have you put it together yet? Do you understand the deaths, how they died? It's not that difficult. You have your own little quirks that you did to the women you brutalized when you kidnapped them."

He thought about it hard, not sure what she was talking about, but then it hit him. "Their fetish. The things that they would do to the women. After they were dead." She said bingo, like they were playing a game and he'd won that round. "You're doing this?"

"Of course I am. I have had training in the art of killing and making others suffer. You'll be happy to know that each of them died screaming out your name as to who took the women and whose house they were tied in." She looked around, and so did he. "When I'm finished with you, I'm going to burn this place down. It's only fitting, don't you think?"

Her voice was singsong like, as if they were not talking about murder and suffering, but about the newest movie that had come out. When she laughed, he could have sworn it was windchimes. She laughed like a beautiful song.

"Now. I'd tell you when I'm coming for you, to murder you relentlessly, but I think this is much more fun, don't you? Keeping you guessing all the time. Having you look over your shoulder to see if I'm right behind you. And, as you can see, I don't need you to be out in the open when I come for you. You will never know I have you until it's too late."

When he woke up, not even sure how he'd blacked out, he sat up in his bed and screamed and screamed. The dicks, they were all there and lined up on his own bare dick like some sort of sexual toy to be used. Christ, he was going to kill himself.

"No, you won't." He looked around for her, the voice seemingly coming from everywhere. "You can't kill yourself, Troy. I thought that I made that perfectly clear. You will die by my hand, and only mine. You have a nice rest of your life. And remember, I'm watching you."

~*~

Mas had been asked to come and see Mabel. He'd not wanted to, and when Adrian said he'd go with him, he felt marginally better. But to see this woman after what she'd done to Angus made him want to hurt her in ways that even scared him a little.

"Mabel, what is it you want? I'm a busy man, and I want to be home for Christmas Eve dinner." She stood up, and he thought that if orange on any other person could look worse, he didn't know how it could. "Well?"

"I want you to bail me out of here. Right fucking now, before I tell the world what sort of person you are." He asked her what she meant. "You know. You beat me and my little boy. And don't think I haven't figured out that you did something to me to make me think that I saw all that shit either. Nor was that Angus. I never thought I'd say this about you, Mas, but you are a cruel heartless fucking prick."

"I see. And how is it that you came to this conclusion? Because if we're making up names for us, then that would mean that you're a nice person that has had bad things happen to you." She told him that was it precisely. "No, it's not right. You're a murderer, Mabel. An abusive mother to Angus until you wanted something. You're a thief, a liar, and someone that I'm very happy to have out of my life once and for all. To think that in all the years you threatened me with my love for that boy, you never once thought of anyone but yourself."

"So? Who else is going to care for me but myself? And since you were caring for my little boy, what other commitments did I have but for myself?" Mas couldn't believe what was spewing from her mouth. She seemed to think she was justified in what she'd been doing. "Mas, I'm not kidding you. People will paint you in an ugly picture if you don't do as I say and get me out of here."

"And who do you think they're going to believe, Mabel? You? Doubtful anyone would believe you if you said it were raining and everyone was standing in the downpour. No, you have made your bed, now you can lie in it. I'm finished with you and your blackmailing me." Mabel told him she was going to ruin him. "That was your plan before you tried to rob the bank. As it is now, you'll be lucky if you ever see the light of day again."

"You lie." He only crossed his arms over his chest, feeling much stronger about this than he had before. "Bail me out, and I'll sign custody of Angus over to you for two million dollars. You owe me that much."

"I owe you nothing. And I don't need for you to sign custody of a grown man over to me. Angus is nearly twenty-seven years old, Mabel. He's more than old enough to be making his own decisions, as well as his own way in life." Mas knew that Mabel didn't have any idea how old Angus was. He'd seen the gifts she'd gotten him when the car she'd stolen was searched. "What did you hope to get by buying him toys and games for a child one quarter of his age? I assure you that once we figure out if you stole them or not, we'll pay whatever is necessary and they'll go to a very deserving child."

"They have nothing on me. A few pictures that could be anyone they want to pin shit on. Once I get out of here, I'm going to make you pay." He'd had enough, and turned to leave her there. "Mas, if you walk out of here, I'm going to kill you when I get the chance. I swear to you, you're going to regret this."

"I already do."

Mas opened the door and made his way to the next door that led out of the building. He could still hear her screaming at him as the doors shut behind him. More than likely, he thought, it was just the things that she'd already said to him that he was hearing. Such things to say to him after all he'd done for her.

Sitting on the stairs leading up to the police station, he sat there thinking of what had happened in the last few weeks. Too much, he knew, but there didn't seem to be anything that he'd not been able to come out ahead on. On the twenty-sixth he'd be heading to Chicago again to help in the apprehension of Allen White. But before that, they were going to talk to his father. Big Al White was not going to be a happy man when this was all over. Mas knew that he wouldn't be if it were his son doing this.

Standing up, Mas made his way to his car. It had been

very generous of Adrian to give him not just a place he could live, but also transportation when he wanted it. Just yesterday he'd helped him change his will around so that Angus would get the business after he retired. Mason had come to him yesterday morning to tell him that she wanted Angus to have it all, as she would be very busy with her own family from now on.

"And besides, I think he'd do a much better job than I could now. I'm so enjoying being the soon to be wife of Adrian." He laughed, never having thought he'd hear those words from his only biological child. "And I'm sure that as soon as you are a grandda, you'll be more than happy to turn it over to him."

She was right—he would be.

Driving out to the site where his new business was going to be housed, he watched the men working. He would never have thought that so much would change here overnight. But he had walls up, as well as power and heat to the place. And the other buildings that were going in were at a nice clip too.

Going to the mall was going to be a nightmare, he knew, but he wanted to get the rings that had been his mother's from the jeweler. He was having them cleaned for Mason, and having his father's pocket watch repaired to give to Angus. Things he knew they would treasure as much as he did.

Having lunch alone had never been anything that Mas enjoyed. He was a man that enjoyed not just his food, but the company that went with it. So as soon as he sat down with his lunch, Mas was thrilled to death when Ollie sat down across from him with his own lunch.

"The women threw me out. What a thing to do to an old man." They both laughed. "I'm to understand that I might have had it right in getting in the way early so I could be tossed to the curb. They're having one of them bridal wakes for Mason."

"Bridal wake? Don't you mean shower?" He said it was all the same to him. A way to get together, drink, and have some good food. "I suppose when put like that, it's what it is. The kids are going to hold off on their honeymoon until after the second week in January. Do you know why?"

"Yes, sir, I do. The place that they'll be staying in, it was hit by one of them storms they had out there." Mas hadn't heard that. "Not that they'd not have as many places as they wanted to go to, but Adrian wanted to take Mason to Paris, and nothing else would do. Are you gonna go with that giving her away with my son, Oliver?"

"Yes. I didn't even consider being upset about it, like Oliver thought I would be. I think that it will be wonderful to be a part of this family in any way that I can. And I have to tell you, Ollie, having someone with me might keep me from bawling like a little baby about it. I'm just coming to realize that Mason is all grown up."

"She is at that. I love that girl as much as I would any of my own should I have had any. Eve, she's just about the best thing that could have come to us when she married my son. And the time after my own wife died, that woman beat me up so much that I had to live." Mas asked if she was violent. "Not her. Not physically. But she sure can peel the paint off a barn door when she has her skirt all twisted up."

"Yes, your sister has a good handle on that too." They both laughed when Mas put his hand to his cheek. "I love this family. You've all given me something that I might not have had had you not stepped in and saved my daughter. I can't think of any way that I can repay you, so I won't even try. Only to say thank you, once again, for being with her when I couldn't."

"You were with her, Mas. Why do you think she jumped? Her only thoughts were about you and how much she loved you. Don't think that she did this out of selfishness. No sir, that's not why she did it at all. She loved you, and she knew that you'd feel bad, but not nearly as much as you would have watching her suffer through that disease." Ollie shivered. "I've heard tell of how those people end up dying. I'd not wish that on my worst enemy, I want you to know."

They talked about this and that, never bringing up what his Mason had done. But Ollie was correct, he could see that now. Mas would never have survived watching Mason struggle through that illness that would eat her alive.

"I got me some shopping to do. Hate to do that stuff, but I surely do love to watch the people doing the last minute jig in getting the perfect gift." Ollie looked so sad for a moment that Mas found him wanting to hug the older man. "I'm going to go and get my missus a little gift. Not much, but I think come spring I'm going to plant her some poseys. That little faerie of Tanner's, she said she'd help me."

"Flora, is that her name?" Ollie nodded. "Yes, I met her yesterday when she came to tell me that I needed a faerie. I have to decide which one I want. I have to tell you, Ollie, that's about the strangest thing I've ever had to do."

"Yes, I can see that. Was for me too, if I was to tell you the truth." Ollie laughed. "She told me that she'd pick me a brownie to use. They got themselves more energy than a faerie, and he'd be able to keep up with me. Plus, old Burt, he's an old feller like me, and we get along just fine."

They walked around the mall, looking mostly at the people instead of the displays they had. Ollie told him that he'd be bringing his grandbabies here when they were old enough so that he could watch them with the pretty colors. He also told him that he was saving up memories every day to tell his dearly departed about.

Going home that evening to pick up gifts to take to Adrian's home for Christmas Eve, Mas felt better than he had in a while—happier, he supposed. Spending time with Ollie had helped him put things in perspective, as well as given him some hope for the future. Like grandchildren. Mas thought he'd enjoy being a grandda to some babies of Mason's, and even Angus if he was inclined to find him a wife too.

Chapter 8

Adrian came hard and suddenly. His body felt as if he'd put his cock into a live circuit and it shook his world. Looking down at his body, he watched as Mason moved up it, kissing his heated flesh as she went.

"Merry Christmas." He laughed and told her that she gave the best gifts. "Thank you. I was glad to see you here when I woke up. Is it because the house is full and you thought you could slip in under the radar?"

"Yes—that's what I was hoping for, anyway. Christ woman, if you wake me like that in the White House, I'll never get anything done." She giggled, and he rolled her to her back, his body over hers as she wrapped her arms around him. "Are you okay now?"

"Yes. I guess last night was just too much for me. I mean, I'm happy. I don't think I've ever been this happy, but having such a big family here, all the laughing and teasing, it just was too much for my heart, I think." He told her that he understood. "You think your family is regretting me coming to this family?"

"Yes, that's the first thing that Mom said after everyone started to follow you to figure out what made you cry and suddenly leave the room. Oh, and my dad, he wanted to cuddle you in his arms and hold you to make it all better. That's exactly what they thought after that. You weren't for us." He laughed, and she smiled at him. "I love you, Mason. And so does my family. You're the best thing that has ever happened to me, and to all of us too."

Adrian slid into her, her heat and scent calling to him. When she moaned and wrapped her legs around his hips, he took her slowly, touching her with his fingers and his mouth every place he could reach.

"Your family will be here soon. Yes, that's it, Adrian. Right there is where you can make me scream." He touched his tongue to her pounding pulse, then bit down. "Adrian, please, don't tease me anymore."

"I love teasing you, love. You make the most amazing sounds, and your breath takes on a new sound when I do it. Like when I kiss your nipple—you shudder, then you inhale sharply." He did it and heard the most erotic sounds coming from her body. "You are almost too much for me at times, but I'd have it no other way than this."

Adrian made love to her slowly at times, then quicker just to catch her off guard. Mason's tiny releases were enough to sustain him for a little while, but it made her needier, her scent stronger. And when he cupped his hand around her tight muscled ass, he pounded her harder than he knew that he should have. But the reward, her screams, were enough to make the little pain they'd have all the more worth it.

"Come in me, Adrian. Please. I need to feel you come deep inside of me." He didn't want to. Adrian wanted to hold off, to wait until she came several more times. Then she did the most incredible thing—she bit down on his throat, drew him into her, and he let go with a shout. "Again, please. Again, Adrian."

He wouldn't have been able to stop his body from filling again, not with the way he felt right at this moment, having his love, his mate begging him for more. As Adrian came a second, then a third time, the air in the room seemed to disappear. His heart beat so hard, so quickly, that he was sure he was having a stoke. And when she came, bringing him to the highest peak he'd ever been, Adrian fell over the topmost point and didn't remember landing at all.

Waking later in the morning, Adrian reached for Mason only to find himself in the bed alone. The pillow was cold, so he knew that she'd been up for some time. Reaching out to find her, he knew that she was in the kitchen with his mom, and had to smile. Even from here on the third floor of the house, he could feel her frustration.

Your mother is driving me insane. He laughed and asked if she'd said that to her. *No. Do you think I'm stupid? How did you sleep? I don't think I've slept that good in ages.*

I slept well too. Thank you so much for the early gift. Mason laughed and asked him if he was coming down soon. *Yes. I'm just finishing up my shower now. I'll be down soon. What do you need done that I can help you with?*

Get down here.

He laughed again as he wrapped the towel around his waist. Getting his clothing from his bag, he dressed and continued to laugh as he made his way down the stairs.

At the landing, he stopped and took in the house that was beautifully done up for Christmas. The tree at the landing was bright with lights and decorations. He would bet that at night, you could see it for several miles. Going the rest of the way down the stairs, he marveled at the garland, wrapped with ribbon and lights, on the bannister. Adrian loved the way it was interspersed with large green and red ribbons.

Standing in front of the tree in the front open area, he looked the tree over, and that was when he noticed that it moved, and the ornaments seemed to be very shiny and shimmery. Hearing a small sound, he turned to look at Kyle, Evan's son, while he stood beside him.

"Did you put out your hand yet?" Adrian said that he'd not. "You should see it, Uncle Adrian. Just do it. Put out your hand and watch them."

He did as directed, and was happy that Kyle had done the same. In seconds the tree seemed to come alive, the shimmering ornaments moving from the tree to himself and Kyle. Tiny faeries, all of them in several hundred colors that descended upon their hands and arms.

"Look at them. Aren't they about the prettiest things you've ever seen? Great Grandda told me that they're as pretty as a speckled pup under a little red wagon. I don't know what that means, but I think he might be right. Don't you?" Adrian bent down to be at eye level with the young man. "All you have to do to get them to go back is say return."

They not only returned, but they seemed to shimmer more. Kyle then dragged him into the living room where the television was blaring, and there were two games on at the same time. He'd not even realized that his television had picture in picture, and stood watching the two different games while his dad and Mas argued about snacks. Adrian made his way to the kitchen just in time to hear his mother telling someone that she needed to curb her language. He figured that it could have been any one of the women in the room.

"Adrian, your wife is insisting that I be her maid of

honor. Tell her that's not the way things are done." Adrian only kissed his mom on her cheek, and then hugged Mason to him. "I have to be out in the audience to make sure I don't miss a thing."

"What do you think you might miss by standing right beside Mason, Eve?" Carter was mixing up some punch and putting it in empty jugs. "Hell, we're all going to be up there. I thought that was where you'd want to be. Right up there where you can slap the piss out of us if one of us fuck up."

"Carter, would it hurt you, any of you, to curb your cursing until after Christmas? I mean, just one day, and that could be my gift." Groans sounded from all over the room, but he knew that they'd do as she wanted. "Adrian, there is a phone message for you. Andrew had to go to the smoke house and pick up a ham. And Henry is on his way."

Pulling the message off the fridge, he snagged himself some of the green bean salad that his Aunt Bea was making. While he was putting the phone number in the phone, she made him a small plate of food. It was mostly veggies from the tray, but it would hold him over.

As soon as the phone was answered, he stepped out the back door to talk.

"Is this Adrian Whitfield?" He said that it was. "Good. Good. My name is Carl Powelson. I was wondering if you could spare me a few minutes of your time today. There is.... Oh my, there is an upheaval that I'd like to talk to you about. Oh my. This is just horrible. I'm in town now, and it won't take that long."

"You usually work on Christmas, sir?" He said that he didn't, but today was unusual. "Yes, all right. Come over to my house, and please, we'd love it if you stayed for dinner. There will be plenty of food and people around."

"This is why I must talk to you. A generous man. Yes, I'd enjoy that very much. I'm to understand that Henry Cobb is going to be there as well." Adrian didn't say anything, and the man laughed. "Yes, I think you're going to be perfect."

Before he could ask him what he'd be perfect for, the man hung up, laughing. Adrian was just telling Andrew that they were having a visitor when the front doorbell rang, and he opened the door up. The man standing there was none other than the senator for the State of Ohio.

"I didn't recognize your name. I'm sorry." He took his coat and handed it to Andrew. "We can go into my office. But if you don't mind, I'd like for Mason to be there with us. She's going to be my wife in a couple of weeks. The fifth of next month, as a matter of fact."

"Yes, that would be good. Yes, yes, that would be a good thing to involve her as well in this decision."

Adrian went to the kitchen again and asked Andrew to bring him something to drink and a few refreshments.

"What's going on?" He told Mason that he had no idea. When they entered his office, Henry was there, along with his attorney. And so was Mr. Powelson. "Gentlemen, I do hope that you're aware this is my first Christmas with my new family, and that you're shitting on my day with calling meetings."

"Mason, as clever as ever, I see." Henry kissed her on the cheek as he sat down with the other men. "There has been some trouble, and I think this is the perfect time for you to come to see what you're made of."

"I don't understand." No one said anything other than to ask him and Mason to have a seat. "If you'd give me some sort of clue as to what is going on, perhaps I can give you a better answer to whatever this is."

Adrian looked around as Henry spoke. "Mr. Powelson here is stepping down. And in doing so, he can pick the person to take his place. I don't think this is normally what is done, but for this, there are going to be special circumstances."

"Why is he stepping down?" Adrian sat down and pulled Mason onto his lap. "And what does this have to do with me?"

"My wife has left me—for another woman, it seems. But that's not the real trouble. She's having an affair with the senator of Virginia. You might say that I'm getting out while the getting is good. The scandal will ruin me and my family if what she has to say hits the news. And it will, I'm afraid. This way I can take off and hide away before the entire story hits the paper." Mason asked him if he was ashamed of what had happened. "No, no. But since she's thinking to take over my seat so that she and the other senator can meet, behind closed doors so to speak, I'm picking you to take my place."

It took Adrian a few seconds longer to understand what was going on, but Mason got it. She was asking questions right and left while he was letting this absorb into his head. Being senator now, it would cut out an entire year of him having to run for the senate. He'd also not have to run the risk of losing the seat only have to start again to run for the presidency.

"I'll do it." He looked at Mason. "That is, if you think we can do this. I mean, it's a little sooner than I thought, but it would also give me an opportunity to do things now instead of behind the scene in running for the White House."

"If you didn't take this job, I was going to cut you off at the knees and do it myself." They all laughed, and Adrian kissed Mason. "I love you, Adrian, and I can't think of a better man to replace Mr. Powelson in this."

Another hour was spent on swearing him in. Since he needed a witness for this, Adrian asked if they could go to the kitchen and do it. He knew there were people in there that no one would question. As soon as they entered the big room, his mother looked at all the men with him and asked what had happened.

Dad joined them too, as well as Grandda. "I think we might have to do this in a larger room, Adrian. Your family isn't going to be happy about being left out of something so monumental." He agreed with Henry, and they all gathered in the living room where everyone else was. As soon as he stood up, Henry addressed the room. "Ladies and gentlemen, I'd like you to meet the new senator for the State of Ohio."

~*~

Bea made her way back to the kitchen before all the congratulations were finished. It was just too much for her, all the emotions. As she sat there, thinking about her grandnephew, Ollie, her little brother and best friend, joined her in the kitchen.

"Are you all right, love?" She nodded, then shook her head. "Yes, I have to say, I'm right there with you on that one. My grandson is not only getting married soon, but he's the senator of the state. Too much for any one person to take in, I think."

"He's not supposed to be old enough to do any of those things, Ollie. He's still a baby in my heart. All of them are." He nodded, and then hugged her. "What are we going to do now?"

"Whatcha mean, Bea? Well, I don't know about you, but I'm going to get me a bigger house so that them new babies can come and spend the night with me. I'm going to learn how to use a computer so that I can keep up with them a little." She asked him if he was going to let her live with him. "I've been thinking on that. When we talked the other day, I didn't think on this well enough. But we need something smaller, don't you think? I mean, a few bedrooms, but nothing like these kids are having."

"I'd like a nice kitchen too, Ollie. I want to be able to bake cookies like I used to, and some treats for the kids." He agreed with her. And then he smiled. "You bought one already, didn't you?"

"Just the other day I was out with that Sunny—my goodness, that girl is about to pop. But we were out and about, and we stopped by this house that she'd been keeping an eye on for another couple. I guess they decided to stay in Florida, of all places. Not that it ain't a right nice place, but there are just too many old folks down there for me. Anyway, I bought it right up. And you and me, we're going to go over there and have a look-see at what they left behind. She said that it's nice, but outdated. I told her we were too. Whatcha think about that?"

"I have some things in storage that we could fill things out with if you want." He said that would be terrific, as he didn't have squat. "Yes, I heard that the boys bought your house from you. I think those boys would do everything in their power to make you happy."

"You too, Bea, you have to believe that. Why, when I was out with Ivy—I do get around, you know—she told me that she's thinking of putting herself in a garden with tomatoes and stuff. She asked me if I thought you'd be kind enough to help her. She's a city girl, you know." She asked him what he thought was a city girl. "You know what I mean. One of them girls that wear those boots that are useless, as well as fix their hair up in those knots that nobody can figure out."

"Oliver Whitfield. What a thing to say about your granddaughter." When he started laughing, she knew that he was joking with her. Smiling, she smacked him in the arm. "The things that spill out of your mouth are something that I have never understood. But I love you for making me laugh. Now, when can we see this house? That thing with Mr. White is tomorrow. I thought that I'd travel with them to Chicago so that I can do a little household shopping."

"Woman, you haven't even seen the place yet. How you gonna know what we need?" Bea kissed her brother on the cheek and left him in the kitchen while she went to see the rest of the family. Ollie was still fussing at her when she entered the living room.

She'd been feeling old for the last several days. Well, she supposed that she was old. At ninety-six, she did all right for herself by keeping her legs moving and her body in shape. Not that she gained any weight—being a tiger had helped with that. Just this morning she'd found out from her dear friend Tanner that she was going to live forever. To be there for all the children and their children coming to the family, being a part of her life. Be around for when all the good and bad things happened.

When someone wrapped their arms around her from behind, she only had to inhale slightly to know it was Mason. The girl was forever hugging someone. Since Bea didn't know the younger woman well, she wondered if she'd been like this since birth, or only since she'd become a cat. Either way, she was happy for it.

"We'll be living in the White House if things go according to Adrian's plan." She told her that she was happy for her. "I was wondering something, and you can tell me no if you wish. But would you mind coming to visit me more often than the others? I mean, they can come as well, but I'd very much like for you to come and stay as long as you wish, and just be my solid ground for me."

Bea turned in Mason's arms and looked into her eyes, wondering for the briefest moment if she was teasing her. But there was nothing there but sincerity, love, and a little fear. Hugging her this way, Bea had to hold onto her emotions again as she answered her.

"I would be honored to do that for you. And to tell you the truth, I wondered how I could get into the place to see you whenever I wished." Mason told her that she'd make sure that she could get in anytime. "You're afraid."

"Yes. Not of what is going to happen to us when this goes through, but I don't want to be messing things up at state dinners and stuff like that. I've been reading up on the other wives, just to make sure I have a list of things that I'd be in charge of, and it's pretty simple stuff." She laughed. "No, it's not. But I'm trying to convince myself that I can do it. But Adrian wants me to help him out with projects too. Things that we're both very passionate about, things that we can work on while there. For instance, better schools, and daycares for two income parents that are paying out more than they make for somewhere safe to take their kids. Then there is the affordable education for anyone over a certain age."

"You mean old folks like me?" Mason laughed and told her no, she meant anyone over the age of thirty. "And what do the two of you think that'll help with?"

Bea had an idea, but she wasn't sure. Mason told her just what she'd been thinking—to help people get better educated so that they had more skills for jobs. It would also help, Mason hoped, to get people off of government assistance.

"And, we're going to give bonuses to the people who become teachers if they stay in their area and teach for one or two years. We're still working out the details on that. In the meantime, we're working on other projects. Things that we hope will help Ohio, and then transfer well to the rest of the country."

"Those are wonderful ideas. Perhaps you can explain to me why it is you want me so close. Not that I'm complaining, never that. But there is another reason, I'm sure." She told her that she loved her. And that she didn't have any grandparents to help her out when the children came along. "You want to have children, my dear?"

"Oh yes. I don't know how many, but I'd like to have at least five or six. Hopefully not all boys, but a mixture. I don't know how Eve did it, myself. Their food bill must have been out of this world high."

"It was, I'm sure. But they had a nice garden and the fruit trees out back. It was good, too, that they had the boys help them. Blake has been planting more hay and straw that they don't need to help out the other farmers around here." Bea sat down on the couch and patted the seat next to her for Mason. "I'm to understand that your mother passed away."

"She did. I didn't know her at all. And even though her and my dad were married at the time she was killed, there wasn't any love lost. Mom didn't want me, not at all. But Dad persuaded her to not abort me and he'd pay her a great deal of money. I don't know how much it was, but he said it was worth every penny." Bea told her that she was sure that it was. "Angus's mother basically did the same thing to Dad, only they were never married. She claimed that Dad was the father of Angus, even though they'd never met prior to her coming to dump him on Dad. I was small, just a baby then too. But Dad had seen how she treated her little boy, and paid her whatever she was asking. Then I guess she kept coming around. But she's in jail now."

"My goodness, child. No wonder you need a guiding hand. It couldn't have been easy on your dad to raise two babies at the same time. What on earth did he do to manage it?" Mason said that he worked less and took care of them as much as he could. But there was other help too. "I had the deepest respect for your father, and now more so. Land sakes alive, I wish I could have been around to have helped him out. Not that I think he needed it. He did a fine job with the two of you."

"Thank you. I'm sure there are times when he thought that he was in over his head too." Bea just patted her on the leg. She really liked this young woman. "I need to check up on dinner arrangements, then we're going to let the children open their gifts. Whoever thought of the adults opening the night before certainly understood the trouble there would be with so many children and their gifts that would need to be opened and put together."

As soon as Mason left her with another hug and a kiss on the cheek, Eve sat down beside her. She looked like a cat that had caught the bird. When Eve smiled at her, she asked her what was up.

"Why can't I just sit down next to you and be friendly?" Bea just cocked at brow at her. "Oh all right, I was wondering if you would do me a favor and talk Mason into not asking me to be her matron of honor."

"I will not. She asked you already anyway, and you'll do it, young lady. Why, that's about the nicest thing a person can do for someone that's not related to them. Eve, you have to realize how hard that would have been for her. She asked a near stranger to be in a special place with her on her wedding day. My goodness, Eve, she's honored you with this request for her." She huffed at her. "I cannot believe that you'd want to turn this down. You have no daughters of your own, and one that is coming to your family wants you to stand beside her. What is wrong with you?"

"I never thought of it like that." Eve looked as if she were going to cry. "I didn't have a close relationship with my own mom. You know that, I'm sure. So I guess I thought that… well, I don't know what I was thinking other than it was a place for younger women. Not someone like me."

"You're no more an old woman than I am. You do what she needs for this wedding. I'm going to be helping her out as well. She asked me to come see her lot in the White House if they make it there." Eve said that they would. It was a shoo-in now, she thought. "I think so too, but I didn't say that to her. She's nervous now. Poor child, having all this thrown at her at one time, and she's coming through like a trooper. I'm very proud of them both."

"I am as well. All of them, as a matter of fact." Nodding, they both looked around the room. Then Andrew told them that dinner was served. "I don't know about you, but I was about to starve to death waiting on the things to get laid out. I sure hope there is plenty to go around."

Bea wasn't that hungry, but she was going to taste a bit of everything. Mason had done another good thing for this meal—each person was to contribute a dish to the dinner, something that was their favorite and something that they'd cooked on their own. Since the boys had the meats, steaks, pork roast, as well as a ham and turkey, the women did the sides. She had even put in her green bean salad, something that she'd not had in a coon's age, as Ollie would say.

Yes, Bea thought, this was going to be the best Christmas dinner and day that she'd had in a very long time. She also thought they'd only get better from here on out.

Following the rest into the dining room, she was happy to see that everyone had a place. Even the children were joining them at the table. But they'd need to expand this room before too much longer. They were growing up too quickly for her. Bea loved each and every one of them too.

Chapter 9

Adrian sat as still as he could in the chair. He was nervous, if he was honest with himself. This was going to hurt a lot of people. Not to mention, a business was going to be lost over it. Perhaps more than one, he'd been told. And Allen would be spending a lot of time in jail.

Last night Adrian had called to speak to Mr. White. He'd had to tell him what was going on, and how his son had cheated others in the area. While Mr. White didn't know about the actual crimes, he said that he'd figured that his son was up to something. And then he told Adrian that Allen no longer worked for the company.

"He thinks your father-in-law is going along with this, doesn't he?" Adrian told him that he did. "And this other man, David Ward. You said that he was a part of this as well, but dropped out? How involved was he? The reason I'm asking is, since my son hasn't been at work, he has become a model employee. I'm guessing now it was a way for him to keep his job."

"As far as I'm to understand from my sources, he was

only in it at the beginning. But you must also be aware that he did go with Allen to the first two businesses that were shafted." White figured that but didn't say anything. "Mr. White, I don't know what your plans are concerning this, but we would prefer that you let the attorneys handle this."

"My son, he needs to understand how wrong he was in this. Well, he needs to be told that it was wrong. Allen was never one to think that he was wrong about anything. He's an ass, and doesn't know the value of anything. That would include money." Adrian told him that he was sure that he'd understand after this was done. "The other companies, can you tell me if any of them have lost out on this? Other than the sale price that he promised them."

"The box company has moved out, and was counting on the money to move into a larger building and make improvements to it. The other two companies are in dire straits too, but one of them is because of their own issues rather than the expected money." White asked him what sort of straits. "They had no one doing their books when they started, and simply went with that the next two years, hoping to be able to afford to hire someone to straighten the books out. It resulted in them not paying enough in taxes. Employee benefits are in trouble as well. They are having issues with the government, again, hoping to get them off their back with the influx of cash."

"I see. Not that it matters to me that Allen didn't cause this. They were hoping to get things worked out with the sale. I'll help all the companies out. But I have a single request. I'd like for your family to take over my company and move it to the place where Mason Tile is moving to. After you agree to that, I'll put in the apartment complex and pay the local school system to hire more teachers and make improvements in the classrooms." Adrian had a counter offer. "New schools? I can see the need for those as well. There would be plenty of room for them too. Yes, all right. You do that for me, and I'll make sure that the area has brand new buildings with improvements for the kids in this area."

And now here he was with Mas, waiting on Allen to show up at the diner where they were sitting in a private room, for two reasons—they would have privacy when it came to having the man arrested, and they could record everything that was being said, as well as the FBI recording the happenings. Adrian let out a long breath when the door opened and Allen came in.

"Hello. Holy Christ, this is nice. When I asked for a private room a few weeks ago, they turned me down flat. Perhaps you can introduce me to the rest of the people here, Mr. Barnhart." Mas introduced Allen to Adrian and the other man, Don James, attorney for the president. Of course, all he told him was his name and nothing more. "Nice. I have all the paperwork filled out here. All you need to do is put your John Hancock at the bottom there, and we'll have this business finished."

The door opened and two men, men that he didn't know, walked in. Allen looked embarrassed, and asked the two men what they were doing there. Apparently they wanted to make sure this went as smoothly as Allen said it would.

"This is Mr. Courtney and Mr. Camp. They're with the business that is going to put in the new high rises. We're hoping that this will help with the housing problems that are plaguing the entire area." Adrian and Mas both shook their hands. "Now, if you'll sign here, I can deal with them and it'll work out for us."

"All right, I'll sign when you give me a check. Perhaps

you could sign it first, just for me." Mas just stared at Allen for several seconds until he laughed. "I'd like you to sign the agreement and give me the check now, if you please. Then my attorneys and I will go to lunch."

"I'm sorry, what?" Now Allen looked nervous. He looked around the room as if he was trying to find someone to save him. "I'll sign it later, when I get to the office later today."

"Why? I mean, we're right here, and I have a pen you can use. Also, the check—I'll need that before you put your name to the contract. According to your wording, I don't get a check unless there is one with the contract when it's signed." Allen was scared now. His nervous laughter and the way his face was covered in a heavy sweat were very obvious. "Would you like for me to show you where that part is?"

"How did you—? I mean, I just gave you this contract. How would you even know that's in there?" Again, with the laughter that was forced sounding. Allen mopped his face with the napkin on the table. "There isn't anything like that in there. Here, let me sign off on this, and then you can be on your way. The check will— I'll mail it to you. That's what I'll do."

"No." Allen looked up when the door opened. In walked his father and two more men. "My attorney has spoken to your father. You might not be surprised to hear this, but I certainly was. He didn't have any knowledge of this sale, nor of you forcing out people so that you could pocket all the money from the sale of our lands to the hotel owners."

"I was doing this on my own, to…to make the company more money." His dad laughed at him and said he was a liar. "Dad, this has nothing to do with you. Why don't you go on back to your office and leave me the hell alone?"

"When you use my company name and my name in a deal

that is cheating good people, then yes, you can bet that I'm going to be involved. What the hell were you thinking, Allen? Or were you? Christ, this is a major fuck up." He pointed out that he'd not signed anything yet. White turned to the men from the hotel. "I'm afraid you've been lied to, gentlemen. There will be no high-rise put in. I'm sorry about all your time being wasted, but my son is going to pay."

"What do you mean, I'm going to pay? With what? Had you not come in here, passing yourself off as some kind of injured person, then I would have been able to be richer than you." White asked Allen if he was sure of that. "Of course I am. All the others just signed off on this paperwork without question. Now you—you told him, didn't you? You looked over the paperwork and pointed it out to him. Christ, you sold me to the wolves, didn't you? You mother fucker. I fucking hate you."

"Well, that's good to hear. But as for me telling Mr. Barnhart about this? No, I didn't. The others did, who are awaiting money from you as well." The others walked in, their contracts in their hands and anger boiling off their bodies. Adrian watched them instead of anyone else in the room. Each of them had been told what was going on when they arrived this afternoon. Their anger was fresh and still hot, just the way he wanted it. "Son, you're going to make good on these contracts, or you're going to jail. This is fraud. And the worse part of it is, you knew going in what you were doing. Christ, did you not learn a thing working for me? Cheating doesn't get you shit. And now you're millions and millions of dollars into this without any way of coming out on top."

"What if I killed you?" Everyone backed off when Allen pulled out a gun. "If I kill you, I'll have more than enough. And after I have to pay off these fools, who should have read the fucking contract on their own, then I'll have your business and money galore."

"You could kill me, I suppose. The issue with that, however, is you're not mentioned in my will. You won't get shit. Nothing. Nada." White laughed. "You are a fool, Allen. You have been since you were ten years old and you failed at being a simple newspaper boy. You couldn't even make that work."

The police took the gun from Allen and cuffed him. The entire time he was screaming about how unfair it was, how his father had ruined everything. And as he was taken away, Evan and Dylan came into the room; they were going to be the ones that took over the business, as Mr. White wanted them to.

"You did a wonderful, powerful thing here, Adrian. Just perfect, and no one was hurt in it. I'm going to talk to the people with the apartments and see what sort of arrangements I can make with them about this. Also, I've had a long conversation with my attorney, as well as the school board, and they're working up a list of where classrooms are needed, as well as a supply list that they need." Mr. White looked at Mas, then back to Adrian. "And for helping me out with this—and no matter what you say, you did do this for me—I'm going to have an athletic building put in and call it the Barnhart Athletic Home. It'll have a clinic, food for them, as well as several trainers on duty all the time. A place for kids to go to before and after school. The city will thank you for that, as much as I do. You're a good man, Adrian." He turned away, but then looked back at Adrian. "You ever run for president, young man, you'll have my vote. Just seeing you in action with this shows me that you're the type of man to wait until you're needed in a conversation, but you have in no time saved the entire state a great deal of money."

Adrian sat in his chair, no less nervous than he had been this morning. But now, he was nervous for different reasons. He'd just taken down a million-dollar thief, and gotten what he wanted in new schools for the neighborhood. White was also going to give the state a bonus in the form of a place that kids could go after and before school to keep them off the streets. It was, as far as he was concerned, a win-win for everyone.

Standing up, he saw Mason packing up the paperwork that he'd brought with him. He came up behind her and held her to his body. It was comforting to know that she was there for him at any time. When she turned, he smiled at her.

"I'm going to meet your mom and all the other women at the mall. I'm as excited as I've ever been." He asked her about the dress, having no idea if she'd even picked out one yet. "Don't you worry about me. I'm so ready. Have you and the others gotten your tuxes fitted yet?"

"Today at two." He glanced at the clock. "I have plenty of time if you'd like to have lunch with me." He wiggled his brows at her.

"No, you're not mussing me up before I meet your mom and sisters." Adrian pouted, pushing his lower lip out as far as he could. "It won't work. I really do want to do this. So, you have fun with your dad and the men. I will see you later at the hotel. Then tomorrow morning, we take care of Troy. I think that's why I'm so looking forward to this. It'll keep my mind off this upcoming meeting."

"I love you, Mason. And in a few days, the world will know."

Mason kissed him again and then left. He didn't want to let her go—he could feel her pain and fear—but she was right, this would be good for her.

~*~

Troy hadn't been out of his house since the police came and took away the bodies. There had been two here; his friend Sam—who had been killed by the same person who had visited him the other day—and Mathew. Mathew had killed himself. Cutting his wrists and his throat while he finished up their dinner had made it so Troy not only couldn't enter the kitchen area, but neither could he eat anything. Not even the box of crackers he'd been able to snag from the kitchen while the police had been there.

The police had been right in saying that Mathew had killed himself. It was obvious to anyone standing next to his body that was what he'd done. And the fact that his blood had been smeared all over the kitchen, including the noodles that he'd been making, was evidence that he'd done it on his own. Whenever he thought of it, it made Troy's belly flop every time. But it was Sam that hadn't been right, not the way the police had seen it.

"He overdosed, plain and simple. See? The needle is still in his arm, young man." He looked at Sam's body, cut to shit like the others had been. "You should pick better friends, Troy. I think the ones you have right now are dwindling down to nothing."

It had been in the woman's voice, the last thing the cop had said to him. And while he didn't have any idea what the cop had really said, he was reasonably sure that it wasn't that his friends were dwindling down. All Troy did now was sit on the couch, with all the curtains drawn, and wait for his fate.

As surely as he was sitting there, he knew that it was only a matter of time. What little sleep he did get was marred by nightmares of the misdeeds he'd done. More than that, he supposed all the carnage and death was what he was going to pay for. Troy was more than ready for it too.

"Hello Troy, remember me?" He glanced up at the woman, the one that had haunted his dreams more than anyone ever had. Even his father, who had been a bastard and an abusive prick, didn't bother him as much as this one did. "I can see by the look on your face that you do remember me."

"Are you here to kill me?" She looked around the room, moving things here and there. Opening the curtains to look out as if she was going to need backup now that she'd come for him. "You're that one we kidnapped. You are the only one that got away. Are you here to kill me?"

"Yes, that's me. My name is Mason. You don't need any more than that, do you, Troy?" He shook his head, and asked her again if she was going to kill him. "Are you so ready to die? Have you all your affairs in order now that you know who is coming for you?"

"I don't have anything left that I care about as much as I do having this end. Are you going to make it fast? I plead for you to—"

"You have no rights to plead for anything, you fucking bastard." Troy cringed from her harsh tone; the words were true, but the loudness of them hurt his ears. "I'm sorry. I meant not to lose my temper. What would be the point, right?"

"You've killed everyone else. You kept me to the end for a reason." This time she moved to the big picture window, the one that his mom had put a big tree in front of every year. But he'd not. Not even after promising her that he'd put it there for her each year. "I'm ready to die."

"Are you? I don't think you are." She opened the curtain, and the sun streaming in burned deeply into his eyes, so much so that he had to cover them with the pillow. "You've let yourself go, Troy. I wouldn't have known who you were but for the household. I wonder why you've lost so much weight? Was it the memory of your buddy standing in front of the sink with his hands full of linguine noodles, covered in his own blood, that kept you out of there?"

"Yes. Are you going to kill me soon?"

Mason just moved around the room. He followed her with his eyes, seeing how bad the room had become. Dust was thick on the picture frames that his mother had taken so much pride in; pictures of him and her at a restaurant; the two of them having a good time at the amusement parks they had gone to. Mail was piled up in front of the door, the mailman not knowing that no one had moved to pick it up. That Troy didn't even move when it toppled over from the size of the pile. Even the couch that he sat on was thick with dirt, the little flakes of it dancing in the air like snow was piling up inside of his home.

"I thought of nothing but you for a long time, before I came to the realization that you're not worth it. I nearly killed myself because you and your friends, all of them dead now, infected me with your disease. Then I met a wonderful family. A man that made me feel like I was worthy of love and happiness. In a few days I'm going to marry him, and all will be all right in my world. But you'll never be a part of any of it, my thoughts or my heart, Troy. Do you want to know why?"

"You're going to kill me. I want to tell you, it's no less than I deserve. I have done nothing but think of everything that I've done in my life, and I'm not worthy of a great many things, especially life." He didn't move, but closed his eyes when she stood in front of him again. "Kill me now, Mason.

Will you kill me now and put me out of my misery?"

"No." He looked at her then, saw her standing up straight and tall, no sign of illness on her beautiful face, her clothing expensive and well kept. "You will die, don't doubt that. But I've only just decided that you won't by my hand."

"The woman from before? The one that I think killed the others?" Mason didn't answer him, but sat down on the foot chair in front of his mother's chair. "I've tried to kill myself. I've cut my wrists, starved myself. Anything and everything I've tried doesn't work. I demand that you put me out of my misery."

"You demand? You have no rights to demand anything of me. Not after the way I begged you to allow me to be let go. The many times that you would promise to leave me alone once you had me one more night. But you never did. You never once allowed me even the dignity of clothing. Of privacy or food. You have no more right to demand anything of me than your friends did. You should have heard them begging, Troy. Heard them pleading with me and my friends to be released, promising over and over that they'd never touch a woman again. Like that was supposed to be something that I'd believe. No, no, you aren't going to be able to beg or demand anything of me. Not ever." She stood up then and pulled out a gun. He didn't stare at it, but at her. "I could end your life right now, and not a person would miss you. Nor would they mourn your passing."

He sat there after she left him. Just left him with her final words, telling him she'd be back. She would too, he knew. Mason would be back several times before he died, more than likely not by her hand. Even though he couldn't kill himself, he knew that he'd be found someday, sitting right here on this couch, his body nothing but dried up bones and dust.

Just as she said too, no one would mourn his passing or even remember his name.

Troy didn't move when he heard the doorbell ring. Whoever was there, like the other times that it had sounded in his home, would eventually go away. Perhaps they'd come back. Or maybe not. He didn't care.

The pounding at the door startled him awake. He didn't know if it was the same day, or for that matter, the same month or week. The bursting inward of the door had him turning his head, and that was when he felt the bagginess of his skin, the way his bones grinded over each other. Even his lips were stuck to his teeth in a way that made him think that they were merging together.

"Troy, are you Troy Forster?"

Was he? He didn't know anymore.

Not answering the man standing in front of him, Troy closed his eyes and closed the sounds of the man's words out. Something about being arrested. For murder. There were names too, of his crew and of the women whose names were burnt in his memory for all time.

"Are you Troy Forster?"

He was moved. Troy didn't have the energy to scream out in pain. He knew that he stank. Getting up to empty his bladder and bowels had been too much for him. While he had no idea how long it had been since Mason had visited him, he knew that these people—there were six of them, he thought—were sickened by what he had become. Passing out, over and over again, he heard someone say that he had no veins in his body enough to use.

Troy was on the road to death, and it was paved with the things he'd done. The deaths that he'd caused and committed. Crimes were there too, of him robbing the local shops only to return the items a few days later to get a "refund." Women were there, some of them nearly eaten alive with the blood disease that he'd given them. Others as beautiful as the day he'd killed them.

Men were lined up on one side of the road, their hands out like he was supposed to give them a ritual hand pat as he went by them. When he glanced ahead, he had to take a second look, then another when he saw his mother there. She was shaking her head at him, the look of disappointment written all over her soft cheeks.

"You killed me, Troy boy. How could you do that to your own mommy?" He shook his head, and told her that he'd not. "You did. When I refused to let you have my pass book to go and take out all my savings. That was for my funeral expenses, you bad boy. I told you that."

"I didn't kill you, Mommy. I promise you I didn't. You're old and mistaken." She huffed at him, just the way she did when she was disappointed in him. "I'd never kill my mommy."

Then he remembered. She'd been upset with him, her walker creaking along the hallway as she'd left his room, taking her pass book—never a bank book—back from him. He'd come out of his room, his body hot with anger that she'd take something from him, and he'd hit her from behind.

The three little stairs that she'd had so much trouble with all his life were right there. Troy had snatched the bank book from her as he shoved his body, much bigger than her frail one, against hers and pushed her down the stairs. And when she landed there on the landing, her body broken and bloodied, all Troy did was curse her as he returned to his room and his latest lover.

It was the next afternoon before he ventured from his

room again, and there she still laid, flies swarming all over her. And when one of them slipped from her lips, like she was spitting the vile creature at him, he threw up twice before stumbling back to his room to call an ambulance for her body.

As he was nearing what he thought was the end of the ride he was on, he cried when it started again. The same people were there; his mother, accusing him of killing her, and again, him claiming that he had not; himself as he knocked her to her death for her money; all the same people, with a few extra added in this time, that while he hadn't killed them directly, he had infected them with his illness.

It was in perhaps its fourth loop when he realized that he was forever going to be seeing this same end of his life. The same people, the same fly buzzing from his poor dearly departed mother's lips. Troy was in Hell. It was the only thing that he could think of, and no less than he deserved.

Chapter 10

The horse was coming along nicely. In a couple more days, Shadow thought that she could have it completed, then she'd be able to start on her next project. She looked around at the door when it opened, and saw her mom coming in the room with two bottles of water that were so cold that the sweat was dripping onto the floor.

"I was in the house, and Mommy told me to bring you something to drink. I didn't know anyone was working out here anymore." Shadow turned her back to her mom to hide the pain of her words. "Do I know you?"

"Yes, I'm Shadow. Your daughter." The woman—because when her mom slipped away like this, she was a near stranger to her—nodded and moved to the other horse that was finished. "Did you see the bead work on his reins? You gave me that idea. I think it turned out very nicely, don't you?"

"I did? Oh." She moved to the other things that were hidden deep in the belly of the big barn. "My mommy used to work at a glass place. They made pretty things for all over the world. Do you know her?"

"I do. She's my grannie." Nothing more was said about her mom. "When I was just a child, I used to come out here and watch you work on pieces that you sold. The shop in town, they have a few of your pieces left that I'm thinking of buying up soon."

"That would be nice. But I don't think that I could have made them. I know nothing about glass. And my mommy said I was too young to work with the glass. I have to be old enough not to be cut all up." Mom moved to the racks that held as many different colors of glass as there were colors in the world, some of them so close in color that it was difficult to tell them apart at times. "The man that she worked for, he would let my mommy order all the supplies that were needed to make a piece of work for his company. Then when he was finished with it—when the run, he called it, was over—he'd give my mommy all the leftover material. I think he was sweet on her."

He was, Shadow knew. The man had married her grandma when she'd been working for him only a few months. But no one at the office ever knew about their relationship, or that Grannie had borne him two children; a girl—her mom, Jaclyn Beth—and a son—Shadow's uncle, Thomas Wayne.

"What are you planning to do with all this? Did my mom say you could have it?" She told her that she had. Every day her mom would ask the same questions, talk about the same glass projects, and Shadow never got bored with her. She was her mom, after all. "That's good. I know that she doesn't let just anybody come out here and play around."

Shadow, a name that her mother used to call her when she'd been a child and under her feet when she worked out here too, was actually Anna Beth, but she doubted that anyone knew that any longer. It had been so long since anyone had even called her that, it was a wonder she didn't go and have her birth certificate changed.

Keeping an eye on her mom, she put the last pieces of the tail on the horse. There were still little things to put together, but the horse, in all his glory, was finished. Now all Shadow needed to do was put the touches of color in his eyes to make him seem more lifelike, as well as shine up his hooves so that he'd be sparkly. Standing back, she surveyed what she'd accomplished.

This was the third such horse that she'd done. They were colorful and whimsical. However, it wasn't the only thing that she'd designed and made while working out here. Some of them were large, others so small that she had set them on stands to keep them from being broken.

The carousel horses would never have a child sit upon them. The weight of the horses would require several men to lift and move them. Their beauty far surpassed anything that she'd ever dreamt of when she'd started playing around with the glass. The glass had been here for longer than she'd been alive, and she would be the last to play in it too, she thought sadly. Shadow had no children, not anyone to love and comfort her. She didn't want to cry, so she worked harder on the piece.

The door opened again. Shadow saw her mom near the racks still, and turned to see her grannie coming into the building. She was pink cheeked and still wearing her large cooking apron, she called it, wiping her hands on it as she moved.

"Shadow? I can't find your mom." She told Grannie that she was with her, and had brought out the water bottles. "My goodness, she's fast. I only suggested that we need to have you more water put out here. I guess she hightailed it out here right away. Well, honey, if you're done out here— Oh my goodness, Shadow. That's beautiful. The colors are...words fail me on telling you how much I love it."

"I like it too. I just have to do a couple more things, nothing but adding some shine to it, then I'll put it with the others. I particularly love the way that the saddle blanket turned out. The way it looks like it's worn in places is something I've never thought of before." Grannie walked to the others and looked at them. "They're getting easier and easier for me to put together too, I think. Well, not easier really, but I'm better at finding where I need to put more reinforcement now."

"And this one, like the others, it'll just sit here in the corner and never see the light of day again?" She didn't reply. It was just something that she did to relax, not for showing, Shadow told her. "You know, you would not need to work that job that keeps you inside so much if you were to simply find you an agent and show off your work."

"No one would care." Grannie huffed at her. Changing the subject seemed the best course of action right now. "I found some of the pieces that Mom made on the Internet the other week. I'm buying them. They're some of her Christmas pieces."

At one time her mom had made beautiful pieces, much smaller than the ones that Shadow did out here. Mom had sold them at a local shop, mostly trees and houses that were snow covered, and very detailed as well. But when dementia started to take away the artist part of her, she'd lost interest in a lot of the things she used to do. So, in an effort to help her remember that she'd once been very artistic, Shadow had bought a few of her pieces. But all it had done was upset her. Shadow bought them now because they had been a part of her mom that she'd lost, long ago.

"Well, if you're not going to listen to me, then come on in the house. Supper is ready. Also, I picked up your dry cleaning while I was in town. My goodness, that place is a mess. I wonder how they can find a single thing in there." They were both laughing as they gathered up Mom and went to the back yard of their home. Her uncle was standing there like he'd been waiting for a while. His mom, her grannie, spoke before she could. "What do you want, Thomas Wayne? I thought I told you to stop coming around here and bothering us."

"What a way for a mother to talk to her son. I've come by to see if you've put Jaclyn away yet. I can see that you've not done a damned thing I've told you to do. Christ, what is it going to take for you to take me seriously? I'm going to be running for the presidency soon, and having that fool around is going to cost me." Shadow told Grannie to take Mom in the house, as she could see that Thomas's words were hurting Mom. Thomas stared at her when the door closed behind them. "Since when do you think I am going to listen to you, Anna? Last time I heard, you were still barely getting around and out of your funk after that husband of yours died."

"Since you seem to have forgotten even the simplest of niceties, I'll cut right to the point, as you have. My husband has been dead for four years. And I've been out of my funk, as you called it, for some time now." He laughed. "I don't know why you think you have a snowball's chance in hell to become president. You can't even get a library card because you owe so many fines. But I will say, if you ever talk to my mom like that again, I will make sure that every newspaper in the world has some of the hateful letters that you've sent here regarding my mother. Not to mention the fact that you've sabotaged everything we've tried to get for her in the way of funding. How could you do that to your own family? Your sister?"

"Easily. I don't want anyone to know what kind of retarded moron I have for a sibling. And they'd not know, if you were to do as you were told. My mother needs to be put in a nursing home as well. She's too old to be fumbling around in this big house with nothing more than you living here with her. Tell her to give it to me, contents and all, and I'll make sure you're getting what you deserve." Shadow asked him what that was supposed to mean. "Christ, do you have to take every little thing I say to you as a threat?" Then he laughed.

"Everything that vomits from your mouth, Thomas, is a threat. And I don't particularly like you." He lunged forward, and stopped when there was a low, threatening growl behind him. "Yes, did I forget to mention that my friend Nate is around here too? He's been keeping an eye on things for me since you decided to try and burn us out. Nate has control over a great many wolves. He's their pack leader. You won't be knocking me around anymore."

"You have to leave here sometime." The threat was there, and Nate growled again, this time louder. "What am I supposed to do, piss myself because you've a bunch of dogs out around this place? I'm not, just so you know. I have a great many people at my disposal as well. You keep acting like this, Anna, and I can tell you right now, you won't live all that long. I hear that lead poisoning can cut short a life quickly. Get it? Lead from a gun? Do you get it?"

"Yes, I get it. Are you five years old? You act like it. Go away, Thomas, before you get hurt. And yes, I'm saying that as a threat so you don't burst that single brain cell you have left in trying to reason it out." He grinned at her. "You're not going to get past the pack, Thomas. I think the only reason you've gotten this far is because they wanted to take care of you out of sight of the street."

Nate moved to stand in front of Thomas. It was then that Shadow noticed that a great many of his pack had been behind Thomas. And now she too was surrounded by even more. When a piece of material was spit in front of Thomas, she saw her uncle pale a little. The blood on it was very obvious, even from where she stood. Nate told her what to tell Thomas.

"Nate wants you to know that the last person you sent here is now rotting in a field on his land. The next time, he said, he won't kill too quickly. His pack, he said, needs to have more practice in chasing down a man and tearing him to pieces." The man was dead, but not by the pack's hands. He'd fallen down a well, and no one had found him until just a few days ago. "You should know, Thomas, that trespassing on pack land will not only get you killed from now on, but Nate said that they're going to take their time tearing you apart the next time he sees you snooping around. I'd take that as gospel if I were you. But then, you've never been all that smart."

"You're going to get what's coming to you, Anna. Christ, I hate you more than I do your mother right now." Shadow didn't bother pointing out that she didn't think there was any love lost between them. "If I don't win this election, you can bet your last buck that I'm going to take the bad news out on you. And my sister and mother. They'll never find out who did it either, because I'm that smart."

"Are you? I doubt that." He started forward again, but stopped when Nate growled again, showing all his sharp teeth. Even his hair stood up on the back of his body. "You're going to have your work cut out for you, it looks like. And Thomas, if you even think about harming my grannie and mom, there will be no place that you'll be able to slink into. I will find you and kill you myself. You can bank on that too."

After he was "escorted" off the property, several pack members snapping and growling at him as he went, Shadow sat down on the ground, her knees no longer able to support her. It always terrified her to deal with her uncle, even when there was help around. Nate came and laid his head on her lap, and while she sat there, she ran her fingers gently through his fur.

Shadow, he's not going to back off this time. Shadow nodded. *I'm going to have more of the pack patrolling your land and the buildings. Also, I'm going to talk to a friend of mine about Thomas. There is something very unhinged about him.*

"Nate, I think he really is capable of being the one that killed Cole." Her husband had been killed by a freak—too freak—accident that had always bothered her in the way it had happened. "Today, I think we saw Thomas's true colors, and it scared me a little."

I'll see what I can do. Just make sure that you're careful on your way to work and home again. I have people there where you are all day, but not on your drive. She nodded. Shadow had been the pack attorney for Nate's dad until Nate took it over. *Why don't you have one of the people you work with ride with you for a few days, to and from work, so that we can keep an eye on you?*

"Do you think that's necessary?" He nodded. "All right. You've been right about him all along, and I'm not going to doubt you now. Also, I don't want to end up in the hospital again."

Thomas had been drunk when he and his buddies had come by her office just as she was leaving for the day. He'd hit her first with his fist in the left eye. Then when she'd fought back, the lessons in defending herself from the pack coming in handy, Thomas drew out a gun and shot her four times. Nowhere that would have killed her, the doctor said, but they'd left her scared to even go to her car without someone going with her. And since he had this ironclad alibi, there was little the police could do about it for her.

When they left her, Shadow sat on the cold ground for a few more minutes, thinking of how hurt she'd been physically when she'd not done what her uncle had wanted. Ten days in the hospital, and even longer than that to recuperate before she could see out of her left eye. Shadow had a few broken bones, mostly ribs, and her face had looked like she'd been run over a few times.

Then when the men had been finished beating the shit out of her, they'd set fire to her car and everything inside of it. Now she had all her papers and notes about Thomas in a safety deposit box that only Nate could get into, besides her and Grannie. Things then had been bad, but she thought that it was ten times or so worse now.

Thomas had sent her flowers and a get-well card that said how much fun he'd had with her. He even signed his name to the card, just to make sure that she knew it had been from him.

Going into the house, she helped Grannie set the food on the table. After Grannie asked for the third time what Nate had said, she told him. Shadow didn't want to worry her grannie any more than she wanted to worry.

"He's right. You take any and all precaution that Nate suggests. All right, child?" She said that she would. "Good. Tomorrow, I need to go into town for a little while. Your mom is going to be at the center. I think I might call that young man up and see if Nate can spare someone for me for a while as well."

After the kitchen was cleaned up, Shadow went up to her room. She had work to do, but not enough to keep her up. But all she did was sit on the window box under her window and look out over the mountain. Crying quietly, she wondered why her uncle was such a bastard. While she didn't have any more answers than she did before, Shadow made note of his visit and what was said, and then went to bed. Tomorrow was going to be a long one, and she wasn't going to be able to work without some sleep.

~*~

Evan joined Nate in the living room to tell him that Dylan was running behind. The man looked worried, and more than that, he was nervous. Sitting down with him, Evan tried to put him at ease, but he wasn't having any of it. The man really was on pins and needles about something. Evan asked him, straight up, what was bothering him.

"I have this friend—we went to school together—and she's been working for the pack for a while now. Anyway, her property butts up against pack land down near Dayton." Evan hadn't known that they had that much land spread out, but nodded. "She's being harassed by her uncle. I know what you're thinking—it's the same old story all the time about human families. You'd be right on this too. But this guy, even Shadow knows he's dangerous."

"He's hurt her before?" Nate nodded, and stood up to pace. "Is there anyone else involved? Children? Husband?"

"No. She's a widow. And today she finally admitted that Thomas—that's his name, Thomas Philips—might have had something to do with her husband's death. I didn't know, but like her, I've suspected it for some time." Nate turned and looked at him, and Evan could now feel his pain. "He beat her so badly about a year ago that it nearly took her life. My dad, he gave her a little of his blood to make sure she made it to the hospital. That's how bad it was. But yes, there is her grandmother and her mom living there as well. The grandma is a hoot—you'd like her—but her mother suffers from dementia. That's another thing that Thomas wants, for them to put his sister away so that no one finds out that he has, and these are his words, 'a retard in the family tree.' Oh, and he's running for president. I don't know his ticket, but I thought that was funny."

"Christ." Nate nodded. And when Dylan joined them, Evan brought her up to speed while Nate took a phone call. "I don't know what he wants just yet, but I'm going to be doing anything in my power to help out."

Nate stood there for several seconds before he turned to look at them. He had a strange smile on his face that Evan found comforting. He had no idea why, but Nate looked like he'd been given the golden ring, as well as the gift card to his favorite restaurant.

"What do you know about showing someone's art to have it displayed or something? The reason that I ask is, that was Elizabeth—Grannie, Shadow calls her—and she said that Shadow is extremely talented, and wants someone to come and see her work. I've not seen it, but Shadow's mom was good at one time, and I've no doubt that the daughter is as well." Dylan asked what her medium was. "Stained glass, her grannie told me. I'm not sure what that might entail, but that's about all I can tell you now. Oh, and she also told me to tell you that she's voting for Adrian. Something about the funding for senior citizens. I'm not sure—she talks really fast. I think Shadow came in the room so she cut me off. Like I said, Grannie is a hoot."

Dylan stepped out of the room and Nate sat down. After asking him what sort of things the uncle was threatening them with, Nate finally came out with what he'd been here for.

"They're a wonderful family, the Philips are. Shadow, her real name is...I can't remember now, but she's been the pack's attorney since she graduated at the top of her class from Harvard. Her husband, Cole Henderson, he was a good man too. Very quiet spoken, but he was smart. He and I used to go fishing together when we were kids. And when he was killed, it really hit everyone that knew him hard. I was wondering if, with all your contacts, you could find out if Thomas did have anything to do with it. I'd love nothing more than to bury him with bad press."

"We can do that. No problem. How was Cole killed?" Nate told Evan what he knew. "Fell from a cliff on their land while out walking? Was he new to hiking around that area?"

"No. And he never went alone when he was out walking. Cole would take long walks with someone and never say a word. He just liked to be one with nature, as he called it. Usually he was with my mom, and she'd be in such a wonderful mood when they returned, simply because he was so easy to be around." Evan said that he sounded like a good man. "He was. Cole also had a good sense of humor. Just like him, it was a quiet sort of humor that would catch you off guard." Dylan came back in, and she and Nate went over everything that she'd need to do a search. "Thanks. I love Shadow like a sister, and she's had a shitty hand dealt to her for some time. I'd like to see something go her way."

After he left them, giving them everything that he could think about, Evan thought about how much he would be happy when his brother Blake was mated. He also wondered briefly if Blake would be a good mate to someone. His brother was enjoying his own life a too much right now, with all his projects going on, to worry much about anything.

"I've just gotten off the phone with a couple of people that are willing to go there and see her work. From what one of them told me, I guess her mom was talented too, but nothing extraordinary, so I was told not to expect much. By the way, I don't know if you're aware of this or not, but she's a young woman. I had it in my head that she was older, like your mom's age." He told her not to say that to his mom. "What? Do I look stupid? She's scary. Anyway, the uncle is a piece of work. And he has some things going on in his office—not sure what he does, but he has an office address—that are keeping his mom and sister from getting aid that they could use."

"You're already taking care of that, aren't you?" She just grinned at him. "All right. So, now that you've told me that she's young, what do you think the chances are that she's Blake's mate?"

"I don't know, to be honest. She's really had a shitty life." She handed him several pages of printed information. "And that's just over the last five years. This uncle, he's going to go down. But, and this will be fun for us all, not before he meets Adrian. By the way, I've taken your tux to the church for tomorrow. Also my dress, along with the rest of them, will be there in the morning. I think there was less involved in taking over a faction in another country than there was to figure out the logistics of this wedding."

"I've noticed that too." Dylan sat down next to him and he thought about his brother, Blake. "The kid that he's adopting will be at his house the day after tomorrow. Also, there are two more boys that he's taking in. One of them has some behavioral problems, but I don't foresee Blake having any trouble with him."

"I heard. They're not related, but they came from the same household." She closed her eyes when he rubbed his fingers up and down her arm. "Evan, do you suppose that he'll fill that house up before he meets his mate? I mean, there are eleven bedrooms in that place. And from what I've been told, he's having work done on the house now that will enlarge the kitchen. I certainly hope this makes him happy. Lately, your mom noticed too, he's been in a funk."

"I did know that. But I think once he gets his greenhouse up and running and he plays in the dirt a little more, he'll be coming around. Also, Adam is selling off his tractors and other equipment so that he can be around working with Blake. They'll make a good team." Dylan didn't answer and he looked at her. "I had no idea that I was so boring."

Dylan had been burning the candle at both ends lately. In addition to helping out Henry, she was also getting things organized for the wedding tomorrow. Security was going to be tight, and he had no doubt that no one would get into the church without having been checked over several times. Evan felt the touch of someone and waited for his mom to speak to him.

I just heard from a friend of your grandfather that he's going to go to Dayton in a couple of days to see some work done by someone named Shadow Henderson. Is that right? He said that while he didn't know when, the rest was true. *I know her mother, I think. Her name is Jaclyn Philips. What does this girl do?*

Other than being an attorney for Nate's pack, she works in stained glass. She told him that was what Jaclyn had done too. *I heard from Dylan that her mother was good, but nothing out of the ordinary. But as a favor to Nate, Dylan set it up for someone to go.*

Do you know if her grandmother is still alive? My goodness, the trouble that she could get into when she was younger. Evan told her as far as he knew she was. Her name was Elizabeth. *That would be her. I might just go down with him. just to visit when he goes. I've not seen them in…well, it's been more years than I'd like to put a number to, really.*

I guess they're having trouble with her son, Thomas. Do you know him too? She said that he was a royal turd. *Yes, well, that's what I sort of heard too. But much harsher wording.*

He goes by his first and middle name, Thomas Wayne. What a moron he was. I thought for sure he'd be in prison by now. Evan told her what he knew. *That sounds like him. When your father and I were dating, he took it in his head that he was going to ruin your grandfather. I didn't know Ollie all that well then, but I'm thinking that it hadn't gone over as Thomas had hoped. You'll have to talk to Ollie about it. I don't know a great deal about that. But Ollie did wipe up the floor with him, I think. Literally, I guess. You talk to him about the man. Are you ready for tomorrow?*

Yes. Are you? She huffed at him. Evan laughed at her. *Mom, have you seen the dress yet? I heard that no one has. I think that Adrian is a little worried that she'll be dressed in a tux like he will be wearing.*

I'm sure she'd look just as lovely as she would in a dress. And no, I've not seen it. I guess she has one, but no one knows what it looks like. To be honest with you, son, I just want this over with. I'm as nervous about this as I have been anything in my life. All those people. My goodness, whatever were they thinking about having six hundred people at the reception?

I'm thinking that they know just what they're doing. Mom told him that she hoped so. Then she said that his dad was home now, and she'd talk to him later. *I love you, Mom. I'll see you later at the dinner.*

Tomorrow his brother would be getting married, and was also going to announce that he was running for the White House. Evan thought that was going to certainly shake things up a bit. Smiling to himself, he knew that his brother, of all the people he knew, would be good at the position. With his wife and mate at his side, there would be little that Adrian wouldn't be able to accomplish. Evan was very proud of his growing family.

Chapter 11

Adrian wasn't nervous. Today was his wedding day, and he didn't feel like he was going to puke on someone, nor did he want to bolt. Marrying his best friend for life was calming and wonderful, he thought.

He'd been nervous last night before going to bed. Today he felt...well, he felt calmed. His body no longer felt like he'd had something hard poured over him to make him stiff. Even his breathing, which at times had been labored and painful, had mellowed out. Adrian felt like a different person—a man who was ready to get things going.

His grandda came to him so that he could fix his tie. "You seen Mason today?" He said that he'd not seen her since yesterday afternoon. "I think you're in for a big one, son. My goodness, she's the most beautiful creature I ever seen. And I hate to say this, but I think she might be more beautiful than your grandma when I wedded her."

"Really?" Grandda looked around, as if someone might have been lurking right around the corner to pounce on him, then nodded. "She never let me see the dress, nor would she tell me anything about it. I was worried. Mason threatened to wear jeans and a T-shirt. Not that I'd care, but Mom would have a cow."

"She's not dressed that way. Beautiful. A lame word, I have to tell you, to describe how lovely she is." He looked at his watch. "Well, I need to get back there. This is about the proudest moment of my life, you know. To be a part of all this."

After a quick hug to all of them, Grandda left them in the room. Even now that it was only minutes away, Adrian felt good. When Henry came up to him, patting him on the back as a way of greeting, they hugged as well. He was going to be his best man, and shield for him if someone didn't want him running for the White House when he announced.

"You ready for this? You're not still afraid that someone is going to throw tomatoes at you, are you? They're not even in season." He said that he was ready, and no, not anymore. Then Adrian told him how he felt. "That's good. Wonderful, as a matter of fact. To be nervous with what you're about to do, then I'd think you were nuts. Mason is a good woman, and will make you a great first lady."

"I hope that I'm not wanting this too badly. I mean, I already am, but I have to tell you, Henry, I'm going to be pretty devastated if I don't get this after all the hype." Henry just crossed his arms over his chest. "Yeah, that's what I got from Mason. Only she tapped her foot too. She's pretty intimidating when she gets like that."

"That is going to get you a great many things done, Adrian. Mason has not just your back, but all of you. She's your temperament. The person that keeps you focused. Not that you've not been that a great deal, but with keeping you focused, she's taught you that it's not always all work and no play. She's a woman that will stand beside you when necessary, but will fight till the death for you as well." Henry laughed. "I have to tell you, there are times when she scares me a little more than Dylan does. And I know what she's capable of."

They both laughed, and the knock at the door told them that it was time. As he and Henry stood at the door, his brothers left the room. This wedding was going to go down as the most nontraditional wedding of all time.

Standing up in front of the massive church, Adrian was shocked at how many people were there. There were even people standing along the edges of the pews, and there had been chairs set up in nearly every open space they could find. It took him a moment to realize that the standing people weren't guests, but secret service. They were here for Henry.

And for him. Being senator had come with not just perks, and a great many of them. But also some things that he didn't find all that nice. Like having someone follow him around everywhere he went.

Adrian had to smile when he thought of the man who had had to follow Mason around. She'd turned on him so quickly and had him down on the floor that he laid there after she'd put him there. When she put out her hand to help him up, he flinched away from her. Instead of debating with him that she was no longer going to hurt him, Mason went and found Dylan. The man was not only off her detail, but was also reassigned to another department.

"If he's going to back off from someone at the first sign of trouble, I don't want him anywhere near the president. And that would include you when you get there. Christ, that was embarrassing." Dylan moved around his office after telling him what had happened. "I'll be better at caring for our family from now on."

And she'd been true to her word. Dylan had been Mason's personal body guard since. And he thought it had made them closer than they had been before. He knew that they all loved her as much as he did. And Dad had a special kind of happiness for Mason.

Adrian looked towards the front of the church when the tempo of the music changed. He was so glad that Angus had found himself a place in the wedding. He'd been asked to be an usher, but had said that playing the organ at his sister's wedding would be the best thing he could do for them. And the man was very good at it too.

Dylan and Evan were the first to come into the large church. Dylan was dressed in the palest color of pink he'd ever seen, and Evan's cummerbund matched it perfectly, as did his bow tie. As they parted, Dylan took her place in the line that would be the rest of the sisters. Evan started behind him, but stopped short of moving past him. His older brother gave him a tight hug. It was unexpected, yet very needed.

David and Sunshine were next, her large belly leading the way, it seemed, as she held onto David's arm as they laughed about something. Adrian laughed too. They were the happiest and silliest couple he knew of all the family members. Her dress was like Dylan's in that it was pale, but it was almost melon in the shade of orange.

Adrian knew that Mason had told them that they could wear whatever they wished. They didn't have to match at all. She didn't want them, she told him, to have a dress in their closet that they'd never want to be seen in again. It looked like the women had gotten together and decided on their own to wear matching dresses. And with the fact that the cummerbunds and bow ties matched the women, Adrian thought they made a wonderful, beautiful choice.

Next was Josh and Carter. They literally glowed when they came through the doors. The dress that Carter had on was a creamy yellow that suited the young faerie well. And the smiles on their faces, the happiness that they showed, was something that he'd never forget.

Adam and Ivy made a stately couple. Ivy, a redhead, could not have had a better color picked for her than the pale green that embraced her body. Her hair, like the others, was hanging down, and he could see small faeries around their heads that formed beautiful crowns.

The last couple to come down the aisle was his mom and Blake. He had wanted to walk a beautiful woman down to the front of the church, and had asked their mom. She'd been so touched by his kind words that she'd hugged Blake for ten minutes or more, sobbing about how good he made her feel. Blake only wanted a small part in the wedding, but Adrian thought that he'd made the biggest impact on their mom. And since Mom would leave the church with Henry, it worked out very well. Again, a nontraditional wedding.

His mom was dressed in a slightly different style than the others, but no less beautiful. Her dress was baby blue. Her hair was done the way that he'd always remembered it, in a long braid that had been wound around her head to form a halo of sorts. And she, too, had faeries in her hair.

When Mom was in line, Blake turned to him with a wink and sat down with Aunt Bea. Even though she'd not wanted to be in the wedding, he knew that she was just as proud and happy to be there today as the rest of them were. Blake put his arm around Aunt Bea, and she hugged him. Letting out a long breath, he waited for the next person to come down to be with him.

His dad came through the door first, then Mas. They both were handsome men, but the tuxedos they had on made them look younger, more stately. If he were to say that to his father, Adrian knew that he'd never hear the end of it, and decided that he could handle it. Adrian would tease his dad for a long time with that.

The music changed. The march began, and everything, including the people around him, faded away. She would be coming now—Mason would be coming through the door and into his life. Holding his breath, waiting to see her, Adrian nearly swallowed his tongue when she came through the doorway, with her dad and his on either side of her.

He would have gone to her had the hand at his shoulder not stopped him. She was magnificent. Her dress, it was beautifully made, but it paled in comparison to the way she shone right at this moment. And the closer she got to him, the more he could see of not just her, but the dress as well.

The sheer lacy sleeves were covered in tiny beads that formed flowers—the exact flowers, he noticed, that she had in her hand; lilies and daffodils the same color as the other dresses. The faeries in her hair, all of them the color of rainbows, dazzled the eye, and their faerie dust sparkled on the ceiling and the large stained glass windows around them.

The neckline was modest—old fashioned, Adrian realized. And when she was standing just below him on the steps, he saw that his father and Mas were wiping away tears as the minister asked them who gave this woman to Adrian.

"We both do." Mas looked over at Dad, and he said the same thing. "I wanted to tell everyone here, I could not have picked a better family for my only daughter than this one. I know that Adrian will protect her with his life, and love her until the end of time."

Mas hugged him and then sat down. Dad looked around the room before speaking. "I had this whole thing planned out that I was going to say, but to see you all here, being a part of this day...well, it's made every word in my head just fly away." He kissed Mason on the cheek. "I love you to pieces, my child. And I'm so glad that I was able to be there for you when you needed me the most."

Dad sat down in the pew next to Blake, still sobbing, but quietly now. And when the minister cleared his throat, Mas hopped back up and went to Mason again. He laughed a little, then handed Mason's hand to Adrian. After another quick hug, he sat down again.

Adrian couldn't help himself; he kissed Mason with all the love he had in his body. The minister cleared his throat again, this time smiling hugely at him.

"I just can't help myself, sir. She's about the most beautiful woman I've ever seen, next to my mom, and I love her very much."

The room laughed, this time loudly and for several minutes. When things quieted down again, he helped her up the step to where he was, and quickly kissed her again, much to the amusement of the congregation again.

"Before we begin to wed this couple, they both have something to say. It is my understanding that they are going to make this short. However, I've known the Whitfields for a very long time, and short is a term they do not use much." Again, the laughter, and the minister looked at Mason. "You may start, my dear."

"Today I'm marrying the best person in the world. As my dad said, this is a wonderful family, and I could not be happier to be here today. I would like to thank my dad for giving me life. Without him I'd not be here—without my father, the man I held other men in comparison to and found them all lacking." She smiled at her dad, then looked at Adrian's dad. "Oliver gave me a second chance at life. When I was at my all-time lowest point in my life, he picked me up, shook me hard, and set me straight. I will always think of him as my guardian angel."

When Adrian was asked to say his speech, he kissed his bride to be again. Then he turned to Henry and hugged him. It was almost too much, the emotions running through his heart right now.

"I've been ordered—yes, ordered—to announce something at this time. Henry Cobb is going to endorse me to take his place at the next election for president of the United States." Hugging the man again, he turned to the minister. "We're ready."

~*~

Mason made her rounds, meeting everyone that had come to the reception. She was almost positive that everyone had decided to come after Adrian had made his announcement. Smiling to herself, she wondered if anyone had expected him to do that, today of all days. Mason thought it was perfect.

Angus made his way to her and she hugged him tightly. "Have I told you lately how much I love you?" She nodded, not sure she could speak around the tightness of her throat. "Also, you might not believe this, but I think people weren't the least bit surprised that Adrian is running for the big house. I just think the way he announced it was the shocker. If I hadn't known, I would certainly have been surprised by it."

"I'm glad to be able to keep people on their toes. I have a favor to ask of you." He told her anything. "I'm going to hold you to that. I want you to tell Dad that he needs to retire—he wants to anyway—and that you're going to run the company.

You're more than ready for it, Angus; you have been for a long time."

It was a good thing there were chairs behind him, because he narrowly missed sitting on the floor. She sat down beside him and waited for her words to sink in. When he finally looked at her with clearer eyes, the first thing he asked her was if she was all right with him running the company.

"Why wouldn't I be? You've been doing it since we got here, and I left you all alone. I actually think you did better than I would have, regardless of what was going on in my head. And from what I heard from Evan and the others, you're doing a great job with it all too. They absolutely love what you've proposed to them. And Dylan said that she's going to have you do some of the offices they have downtown when you're finished with the hotel. You've also been overseeing the new plant that is going in, as well as keeping things in Chicago from falling apart." He told her his real reason for the question. "Angus, you have been and will forever be my brother. My brother—not half, not step, or whatever other people think we are. We're the best kind of family, because we have Dad. And I know for an absolute fact that he doesn't think of you as anything but his son. Biological or not, he loves you as much as if you came from his body."

"He is the best. And I have never been loved as much as I have been with the two of you." They both looked in Mas's direction as he laughed with Henry. "Are you really going to go to the White House, Mason? Be the first lady and all that other stuff? Not that I don't think you'd be great at it, but it will put you in the public eye. And I know how much you hate that sort of thing."

"Yes, well, I love Adrian. And I can do whatever he needs me to do because I love him that much." Angus looked at her when she said his name. "Dad couldn't be prouder of you, Angus, with the way you've been doing this for him. Now I think it's time that you start being the man in charge, so that Dad can hang out with his friends and make new ones. Like you're doing now."

"I am making friends. And I'm going to go out with Ms. Patrick—Ellen—next weekend. We've been meeting for coffee and such a great deal, but I want to see her more in a date sort of way." She asked if he knew she had kids. "I do. Ellen's kids have been hanging around the job site with me. I've put them to work. She came to thank me, and we hit it off very well. Her husband—ex-husband—is out of the picture, so I won't have to worry about him. And the kids, they've responded well to us seeing each other. Not that I've spent the night or anything, but I think we could be good for each other. All four of us."

"That's wonderful, Angus. I'm so happy for you both." He said it was their first date. "I know that you'll have a good time, and so will Ellen. I like her, if that matters to you. She's a lovely woman."

"It does. Thank you, Mason. I think she is as well." Mason held his hand for a moment. "I really thought you'd say something about her being older than me. She is, you know—about eight years. Her kids are teenagers."

"Do you care? Are you happy?" He shook his head, then nodded. "Then to hell with what anyone else thinks. I'm thrilled to death for you both, and her kids. She's a very lucky woman, your Ellen."

When he left her to find the woman that he was sweet on, Mason walked around the room again. She stopped here and there, talked to people that she didn't know, and gave her opinion on things that didn't really matter to her at all. Like what color did she think she was going to paint the master bedroom when she was at the White House.

"I'm sort of in love with white. It goes with everything." She'd seen the master bedroom, as well as all the rooms on the upper floors. They'd been given a tour by Henry himself. The only thing that she could think she'd change was the master bathroom. It was bright orange, a color that Henry's wife adored.

There were other things that they were thinking about, in a funny sort of jokey way. Adrian said he was going to chance the oval office into a square, and take out all the couches and put in recliners. His idea was that everyone should be comfortable when there with him. Oh, and he wanted to have a larger than life television put in so that he would be able to see himself better when he was on the news or something. She said she was going to have the china room redecorated with toys that one would get in a meal for a child at fast food restaurants. Then she'd call it the short meal room. It was fun like this that got them through all the things that were going on in their lives right now. When she thought of it, she realized that things were calming down in that area as well.

Like, Troy was dead. She'd not killed him. Two hours after she'd left him, he'd finally succumbed to his illness, as well as starvation. He'd stopped eating before she'd seen him, and the doctor said that there was no one to blame for his death but himself. Troy had simply given up.

Angus's mother was in prison. Her trial had been short and to the point. Once she'd been identified as the murderer in several of the ones she'd committed on her journey to see Mas, it had been easy for the jury to find her guilty of everything that had been brought out later about her. Fifty life sentences, with no chance of parole. Dad had said that as far as he was concerned, she had never existed, and he didn't speak about her again.

When Mason found Adrian with several senators and a few other people in uniforms, he excused himself from the circle of people that he'd been talking to. When he was far enough away, he pulled her into his arms and kissed her hungrily. She gave as good as she got, and when he finally backed off, she leaned her head against his chest.

"Are you having fun?" Mason nodded and looked up at him. "Yes, how many questions have you answered about us being serious about running for the White House? Not to mention, how many have asked you if Henry is a presidential look alike?"

"The first one, at least a dozen. I told those people that you were such a kidder, but did tell them that we were serious about it, and were looking for funding as well as help in the political arena." They both laughed. "I've not had anyone ask me about Henry. He sure does light up a room, doesn't he? And have you noticed how he drops your name into about every conversation? Oh, and the two new plants coming here, that's been a big deal too. I'm to understand you're going to be working with a couple of other state senators in seeing about getting more businesses to come to their state. Good job, honey."

They didn't separate when people came to talk to them after that. Mason was glad that he included her in queries that people had for him. And when she had a different opinion than he did on something, Adrian said that her way was more than likely right, as she was never wrong. Guests walked away with a smile when they did that, and seemed to be happy that they'd disagreed about something. Mason looked up at her new husband.

"I love you, Adrian." He kissed her on the nose. "This is the best day of my life, marrying you. I couldn't have been happier if someone were to have given me a pony when I was a child."

"Your dad did give you a pony. And when he figured out what you wanted it for, he bought you several more. Giving them to kids in your neighborhood was a wonderful thing to do. And making sure that they could go around to see the sick children was an amazing thing that you did to cheer them up." She felt embarrassed with him finding out what she'd done. "I have something to ask you before Blake has a stroke trying to get our attention. This dollar a dance thing; how about we up it to five bucks a dance, and we tell them that the money will go for the preservation of the gardens around the courthouses all over the state?"

"I love that idea. I mean, even if we only make fifty bucks, that'll go a long way in getting some flowers taken care of, don't you think?" Adrian said she was underestimating her beauty. "No, I'm not. And if we're going to make this work, we should also have you dance with people. That way we can double our money."

The announcement was made, and the first person that paid to dance with her was her father. He also donated a hundred dollars to the cause, and danced the entire three-minute dance telling her how much he loved her. The next dance was her new father-in-law, then her grandda-in-law. After that, it was a blur of who she was dancing with at any given time. But it was fun, and the men certainly made her feel good about doing this for a good cause.

Blake was taking care of the money and lining the people up to dance with them. At one point she danced with a waiter, and all he did was spend his five dollars by holding a tray of food for her so that she could eat something. Her brothers-in-law each danced with her too, and brought her glasses of water, as well as helped her remove her shoes. After three hours of that, the game was finished, and she got to sit down. Adrian, just as exhausted, joined her a few minutes later.

"Excuse me, everyone." The room quieted down and looked at the bandstand, where Blake was talking. "This money is going for a great cause, and I want to thank each and every one of you. We raised just over twelve grand for the courthouse flowers that will be planted in the spring, which is hopefully enough for all of them. Thank you again, very much."

While the gifts were loaded up into a large van, Mason went to talk to her new in-laws. They were leaving soon, only for the weekend, and when they returned, all the gifts would have been scanned as well as marked. The Whitfields were going to keep an eye on things for them while they were gone. Adrian spoke to her dad and brother before they left the reception in the long white limo, rented just for the day.

Chapter 12

Adrian opened the bottle of champagne from Henry. There was a platter of meats and cheeses from the hotel, as well as a basket of fruit, a canned ham, and other items that could be eaten by them without leaving the honeymoon suite that they had for the next two days. Adrian thought that if her sexy nighty looked nearly as beautiful as her gown had, he'd never make it until Monday morning.

"We have plenty to keep us filled up with energy. I think that everyone thought we'd need it to keep up with each other. I wonder where they got that idea." He heard her answer him, then laugh. "Yes, well, it's my right as your husband to put my hands on you anyplace I want. You could do the same if you weren't such a prude. You need to loosen up, my dear wife."

"You think so?" He turned around and simply forgot everything but breathing. "I decided that having an expensive nighty that you'd just tear to pieces was dumb. Besides, I think you like me naked anyway, don't you?"

And naked she was. There wasn't even a ribbon in her

hair, nor any jewelry but for her wedding ring to hide a thing from him. Telling her to turn around, he was delighted to see that she was just as nude from that angle as she was from the front.

"Did I overestimate what you might like from me?" Adrian could hear the teasing in her voice, but he was much too enthralled to care if she was kidding him or not. "You look wounded, love. Did I hurt you? Do you need me to kiss something to make it all better?"

"You are a minx." Mason laughed again. "Come here, love. I have decided that you've broken several areas on my body that need some instant repair from you."

Her walk was dangerous, the way she made her hips sway, her breasts bounce just enough to make his mouth water. Adrian realized in that moment that he'd never seen her cat, even just a glimpse of her. And when she was still a few inches from him, she cupped his cock in her hand and gave him a nice squeeze.

"Mason, we have all weekend for you to hurt me. Hurt me more. Why start out with making me feel like I'm never going to make it for the next hour?" Her giggle, sexy and low, had his cock stretch tightly in his suit pants. "I need for you to undress me. I'm completely at a loss as to how to continue from here."

The belt he had on was the first to go. Adrian noticed that she took her time at removing it, and managed to brush her fingers over his already over tight cock several times before she tossed it to the floor. Next, the snap and zipper to his pants. Holding his breath, Adrian was sure she was going to catch him in the teeth of them just to be mean.

But the zipper slid down on the material smoothly. The motion, however, was lost to him as she licked him from his navel down the entire length of where his pants were now open. Adrian reached out and held onto the first things his fingers brushed over. It just happened to be the bed, one of the four posters holding up the canopy.

Adrian let go of a nervous laugh. He was losing ground here, and quickly. If she took him into her mouth right now, he was going to come. There wasn't a part of him left that could hold onto himself any longer. As his pants moved down over his hips, her mouth followed them. Yes, he thought, she was assuredly going to break him on their wedding night.

When he was in nothing but his shirt and socks, Adrian felt his knees tremble. She was looking at him like he would a fine steak, with all the trimmings. While a man wanted a woman to look at him that way, Adrian found he was just a little afraid of his new wife. Mason looked like the cat that she was, and he was going to be her prey.

"You're thinking too hard. What would you like me to do?" He let the words fall from his mouth unfettered. "You want me to take you in my mouth? I thought that might end you. You said that several times now."

"I did? Perhaps it was my mind shielding me from falling apart in front of you. I will. You've turned me into a mess." She grinned, which Adrian did not find all that reassuring. "Mason, if you don't do something soon, I'm going to beg you. And you don't want to see that. Not tonight of all nights."

"I will if you can tell me one thing." He said anything. "I would like to be fat with your child when you're being sworn in as the next president of the United States."

Adrian would never know where the strength came from to pick her up from the floor. He not only pressed his lovely wife against the wall while sliding deep inside of her, but he managed to make her come twice before he was able to fuck her as hard as he wanted.

"Bite me, Mason."

She did. Her teeth shifted—he could feel the cat in her marking her mate. And when she sucked hard on the wound, drawing even more of him into her body, he cried out himself, emptying deep inside of her. But he was far from finished.

Taking her to the big bed, he didn't give her time to move before he dropped her onto it and put his mouth over her soaking wet pussy. Her screams were like music to his heart. It was as if she were singing a song just for him.

Adrian continued to devour her until she yanked his head up by his hair. Staring at her, seeing the need that he'd put there, made his cock stretch and thicken. Moving up her body, he didn't bother touching what he'd already marked on her. She was his, and would be forever.

"I need you."

Adrian nodded, feeling his cat snarl at him for not filling her. Nipping at her neck, he realized something profound. "You're in heat, Mason."

"I know. I just figured that out. If we have to be holding a baby out there on the cold morning, I can live with that as well. Take me." His cat seemed to tell him get on board with that. To fill their mate with their child. As soon as he entered her, he felt his cat gentle, his body relax. "I swear to Christ, Adrian, if you slow down now, I *am* going to fucking break you."

He laughed, and that set her off. When she rolled him to his back, she rode him like a rodeo rider would a bull. To hell with the bull, she wanted her pleasure now. Rolling her to her back again, it was like they were trying to get the better of each other until they both landed on the floor with a loud thud. Before he would think what she might do to him now,

Mason sat up and started laughing. Adrian joined her when he realized that she wasn't going to beat him to a pulp.

"You're very greedy. Did anyone ever tell you that before? Never mind, don't answer that." Adrian pulled her down for a kiss, and she laid her head on his chest. "How about we start all over, and make love like people and not the animals that we are?"

"Take me right here." She sat up and he watched her move, holding her breasts and playing with her nipples. "This heat thing, it certainly makes me feel like I can't get enough of coming. And even with the amount of times—. Oh yes, that's it. Help me move."

Watching her was fantastic. She was greedy, but Adrian didn't care, so long as she was happy and had her pleasure, Adrian decided that he could simply watch her all his life. But when she leaned down, took his tender nipple into her mouth, and bit down, Adrian came like a roaring animal. He came hard three times before his entire existence simply blinked out.

Waking up, they were both on the floor with covers, sheets and all, wrapped around the two of them. No pillows, he realized when his neck popped twice as he sat up, but Christ, he'd never felt this good in his life. Careful not to wake Mason, he stood up and stretched all the kinks out of his body. Leaning over, he picked her up and put her onto the softer mattress.

"I love you." He kissed her on the mouth when she spoke to him. "I think that we might have to tip someone a great deal after the mess we made. But right now, I don't care."

He looked around the room after putting the blankets on her. Adrian could see that she was right. They had made a mess of things. While he didn't remember waking up, they must have gotten into the fruit basket, as well as finished off the bottle of bubbly at some point.

The cheese and crackers were opened too. Crumbs led him to the bathroom, where he could only stand and stare. There were more crumbs in the tub, and to him, it looked as if they'd had themselves a picnic at one point, because the ham had been eaten like it was a sandwich, with crackers stabbed into it for some reason. Laughing as the night came back to him, Adrian cleaned up their mess enough that he could shower.

While he didn't have any plans today other than to be with Mason, he knew for a fact that he stank. After last night, he didn't think either of them would be all that fresh today. Using the stuff in the bathroom rather than getting his own things, he held his head under the spray. Adrian wanted to clean out the rest of the cobwebs he thought might still be there.

When Mason joined him in the shower, she scrubbed his back. The loofa was hard, but it felt wonderful on his back. Mason told him that she was sore, and he'd known that she would be. The kind of sex they'd had last night was almost too rough for him.

"How about we get dressed, then go to a couple of places and be a married couple? I know there is an art museum here, as well as the North Market. It's a blast to go to. Maybe we can pick up some lunch there as well." Mason told him that she'd love that, and asked about any antique malls around. "Yes. I think there might be a few. You looking for something?"

"Dylan asked me to find some old pipes for Evan. His birthday is coming up soon, and she said that he loves them." Adrian had forgotten that—that his brother's birthday was soon, and that he loved pipes. "Dylan got him a display case for them for Christmas, and he had three open spaces. One of them is for this one."

She showed him the picture, and he knew that it was something that his brother would love. He didn't know if anyone would have it in their shop; he also figured that, even if they did, the chances of finding that one would be very slim.

"We'll ask the front desk." He looked around the room when he was finished dressing, just waiting on Mason to find her shoes, and smiled. "You were right about the tip. I think we did more than some young kids on spring break."

As they were leaving, he laid two hundred dollars on the dresser, with a little note saying that he was sorry. But she took the note back and put it in her purse. Adrian didn't ask her about it until they were in the elevator.

"You signed it. What would happen if someone was looking for some dirt on you and found this note? 'I'm sorry about the mess we're leaving you here.' Then you signed your name. That could mean anything. Or, what I mean is, they could make it mean anything. I mean, I don't know for sure, but I'm thinking like Dylan. That, of course, could be good or bad, now that I think of it."

"I think you might be right." He kissed her. "It's a good thing that I have you in my life. You keep me on my toes and out of jail."

They made their way to the market first. There was so much more to see in Columbus than at home, but he loved their little town. The man at the front desk at their hotel had told them of several antique places that were a little off the main path, and they went there after eating lunch.

All in all, it was an amazing day spent with the woman that he loved. They spent money when they wanted, haggled on things at the antique store, and ate food that would be considered bad for them.

~*~

Blake had a feeling that he was being set up—to get a mate. The woman that he was meeting at the restaurant had called and said that she had a few plants that she needed identified, and she had even given the name of a reputable landscaping business. Blake was still getting supplies in for his own place, and said that he'd meet her there.

The little bistro was busy, even for a Monday. Playing with the hummus that he'd ordered, as he'd skipped lunch again, he dipped his naan in it and looked around. This place was someplace that he came to often, mostly as pick up orders, and he knew that the couple that owned it were looking to expand. Hannah sat down across from him, the wife of the owner, and handed him a few papers.

"You know that we're busy enough to expand—you've been telling us that for months. I finally convinced Howard that we need to do it. I pointed out how many people were turned away because of the long wait here." He didn't even glance at the paperwork. He knew what it said. Adrian had drawn it up for them several months ago. "It's a lot of money, Blake. If you turn us down, I can completely understand that."

"I have no intentions of turning you down. In fact, I have a better idea for you. I think you should open a second restaurant. Then turn this one into pick-up and delivery." Blake waited for that to sink in. "You already do a good business with pick up now, don't you?"

"Yes. But to have two places…? We're already working ourselves to the bone now." He pointed to her daughter, Megan. "You mean let her run one of the places? I don't know. She's kind of young, don't you think?"

"Young or not, Hannah, she is the one that came to me

about this proposal. She thinks, and I agree with her, that you could double your money in a month, pay off what you'll borrow from me, as well as help out some of the kids around town by giving them jobs. I know for a fact that you already have several of the football players in the back right now washing up and doing the cleanup." They both watched Megan as she joked with a customer about the long wait before seating them. They seemed to be in a much better mood by the time she got them to the table. "She's a natural, just as you and Howard are. And she said that running the restaurant for you would be her best dream. Did you know that she's been taking classes online and at night to earn a business degree?"

"No. I mean, I knew that she was going to school, but...I've been missing a lot of things doing this, I think. She is good." Hannah turned back to him. "I'll talk to Howard, but don't expect too much from him. I think he's about ready to cry, I kid you not, Blake."

A woman stood by the table, and Hannah and he both stood up. He didn't know what the woman he was meeting here looked like, but Hannah seemed to know her. She explained how they were business partners.

"I see. Well, I guess that's all right." Hannah looked at him with a cocked brow. "I mean, who meets a woman for dinner, then has someone else at his table?"

"I'm sorry, I didn't realize this was a date, Miss Morris. I was to understand that you just needed help identifying some plants. If I have that wrong, then perhaps we should part ways now." She just stared at him, then at Hannah. And when she told Hannah to go away, Blake was pissed. "I'm leaving as well. I have better things to do with my time than to sit with someone that has the manners of...never mind. You have no manners. Good night. Hannah, if you don't mind, I'll take something to go."

"Now wait just a fucking minute." The room turned to stare at them. It was so quiet that he could hear the woman's heartbeat. "I was told that you were a nice guy. You're a fucking prick. I don't need this shit either."

"Excuse me then." As Blake was walking away from the woman, she grabbed him by the arm and turned him, knocking over the table and all the things on it. "What do you think you're doing? Let me go."

"No. I'm having dinner with you, and you're going to be a lot nicer to me than you have been. I don't know who you think you're dealing with, but I don't put up with shit like that from men." He picked up her hand from his arm and let it go. Blake was embarrassed right now, and since he didn't deal with confrontations well, this was making his cat a little crazy. "Now, you sit down and be nice. Understand me?"

Anyone close to me? I need help at the Little Bistro. After calling out to his family, he kept an eye on the woman. His dad said that he was just in front of the restaurant now. *Please come to me, Dad. This woman that Mom wanted me to help is unhinged.*

It wasn't until Dad was standing with him that he stopped laughing. Miss Morris was yelling at him, in a very loud voice, that he was going to be nice to her. While he didn't have any idea what she thought was going to happen, his dad said that he'd called the police.

"What the hell did you do that for? When I got here, my date was entertaining another woman. What was I supposed to do? Let him get away with that?" Dad asked her who it was she was dating. "Him. Mr. High and Mighty. Christ, this is a shit storm. I got all dressed up, excited for our date, and he fucks me over."

"I was talking to Hannah about expanding." Miss Morris huffed at him. "Dad, I swear to you, this wasn't a date, but me helping her out with some plants. That's all it was."

"Your mom, she's coming too. She said she wants to see if she can fix this." Miss Morris was still talking a mile a minute, saying the same few things—she'd gotten dressed up, they were on a date, and that he'd screwed her over. "Mom said to make sure you don't leave here without witnesses. I'm surely glad that you called me. My dad is on his way too."

This was a nightmare. People were ignoring their meal in favor of watching them. Blake stretched his neck, trying his best to calm himself. The popping sound was loud enough to make Miss Morris stop talking.

"Did you just fire a gun at me?" Before Blake could speak, she started hitting him. Blake didn't touch her, making sure that his hands were behind his back so that it wouldn't come out later that she'd been hurt by him. "I will not take that. Do you understand me? And when I agreed to marry you, you said that you'd not hit me again."

The police arrived just as his grandda did. Aunt Bea was with him. Before anyone could help him out of this situation, Grandda put his fingers in his mouth and let out an impressive whistle. No one moved.

"Now, you calm your butt down right now and have a seat. You're off your noodle, woman, if you think that my grandson here would marry a nutball like you." The room started laughing quietly, but Grandda wasn't finished yet. "You sit down, young lady, or so help me, I'll have you arrested. I might just anyway. Look what you did to Blake. He's got himself a bloody nose and a busted-up lip. And here you stand with nary a speck of dirt or blood anywhere on you. What is your deal?"

"My deal is that he asked me out to dinner again, and I accepted. Then when I got here, he had another woman sitting with him all cozy like. I won't put up with that after we're married." Grandda asked her if he'd proposed. "Not yet. He was planning to do that tonight. I saw the ring."

While Blake tried to digest what she could be talking about, Aunt Bea took over. "This man, the one that was to propose to you, what is his name, child?" The woman looked around, clearly confused. "You take your medicine today, Miss Morris? If you tell me where it is you're staying, I can fix you right up."

Miss Morris put her hands to her head. "I'm feeling better, and I stopped taking them. Who wants to feel like they're all doped up all the time? I feel just fine."

But she sat down then, holding her head as she repeated over and over that she felt all right. Blake moved when Aunt Bea asked him to, and she sat with the obviously ill woman. Blake didn't leave, however. He was actually afraid to now.

Aunt Bea asked one of the police officers to have a look in the woman's purse. They pulled out several prescription bottles, all of them in her name, Trinity Morris. There was a gun too, and not only was it loaded, but there was an extra box of ammo to go with it.

It took them ten minutes of talking, his aunt and Trinity. But she calmed a great deal, and the police were able to get in touch with her doctor. He said that he was on his way, and that he'd explain when he arrived.

Trinity was taken to the hospital a few minutes after the doctor got there, and his Aunt Bea went with her. The medic said that he'd keep an eye on Aunt Bea, but he was sure that the woman was going to be all right with her there.

"Several years ago, she was dating a man. He was all set

to propose to her, she had that part right, but a gunman came into the restaurant and killed him. Trinity saw him do it, and her mind, already a fragile thing, just couldn't deal with it. She's been under my care since then." Blake asked the doctor if she was going to be all right. "She will, I believe. It happens more often than you might think. A patient will feel better—dealing better, I suppose, is a better way to put it—and they stop taking their medication. No matter how many times you explain to them that it's the medication they're taking that is making them feel better, they just stop. This time she was lucky to have been with you and your family. Sometimes when a patient gets too unpredictable or angry, the person hits them, or worse. Thank you, Blake. You did all the right things with this. Few would have, I think."

Blake bought dinner for everyone in the restaurant because he felt so badly about what they'd seen and heard. As he took a meal home for him and Bennett, his soon to be adopted son, he thought about what the doctor had said to him. He wondered if it was something that Adrian could help out with.

Bennett Floyd, a fourteen-year-old, had come to him one cold night a few days after Christmas. Blake had only just put in his application, to be a holding place for children that needed to be in a safe place, that morning. Two days later, it was determined that Bennett wouldn't be able to return to his own home, and Blake asked about adopting him. Benny, as he liked to be called, was all for it.

"Having a warm place to sleep and food all the time is great. Not to mention, not once have you ever hit me." Blake told Benny that he never would either. He'd make his mom do that. Benny had been calling his mom Grandma since the first day, so he knew enough to be frightened of the threat.

Benny was sitting at the table doing his homework when he got there. Noreen, their cook, asked for the night off, and Blake was glad to see that Benny hadn't gone to bed yet. Having the younger man in the house with him made it seem less lonely. In a few more days, his second son would be joining them, and both he and Benny were excited to meet him. They had a feeling that Joey was going to fit right in too.

Chapter 13

Adrian was just looking over a contract that Blake had wanted drawn up when he heard from David. Thinking that it was about his book being finished up, he stood up when his brother started screaming at everyone to come quick.

The baby. She's coming. She's coming right now. Mom, calm and cool, asked him if he was at the hospital. *No, she's on the stairs. Sonny is, not the baby. But she will be soon. Oh Mom, she's going to have the baby right now on the stairs.*

Laughing at the way the two of them were talking, Adrian picked up his coat and said he was on the way. Mom was so calm it was relaxing him, while David seemed to be off the deep end with fear.

The sudden quiet scared him a little, and he paused at opening the car door. He was afraid—not for the child; she was immortal—but for his brother. Adrian was fearful that his brother had fallen down the stairs or Sonny had pushed him. When he finally spoke again, it was like he was hearing an entirely different person this time.

I'm all right now. Sonny is in her bed—she put herself there.

After she smacked me. Everyone laughed, and Adrian could hear the relief in their laughter. *Her mom and grandma are here now, and things are moving much better. I'm sorry, everyone. I've never been a father before, and it freaked me the fuck out.*

I'll allow that this time, young man, but watch it around my great-grandniece. David said he was sorry, but he was concerned about Sonny. *As you should be. But cursing isn't going to make things better, now is it?*

Bea, I swear to you that you have the most impeccable timing. And if you didn't get that, I was being sarcastic. My goodness, woman, let the boy go on and tell us how they're doing. Quit your harping on him about his language. Damn it all to fuck and back. Everyone burst out laughing, because Grandda never cursed. But this time, he was absolutely perfect with it. *You kids get on over to the house. I'm going to have me a louder conversation with my sister here.*

By the time Adrian arrived, Mason was already there. She'd been out looking at the new plant with her dad and brother. It was coming along, she told him after a quick kiss, and they entered the crowded house holding hands.

The place was a complete mess. Mason had been saying just this morning how she didn't like clutter. She was good at leaving it on her desk, but no one was to touch it. She claimed that she knew just where everything was, and she could find it in seconds. So when she put her fingers in her mouth and let out a shrill whistle, everyone turned to her.

"This is not helping them upstairs. Eve, can you go in the kitchen and see what can be done for snacks or lunch? Dylan, if you'd be so kind as to organize the kids someplace other than where they might hear something they shouldn't." Mason glanced at Grandda, but said nothing. "Evan, I'm sure that they won't need your help, but if you could go up, as a doctor, and let us know how they're doing, that would be great. Josh, you take David outside before he pukes on the carpet, and help him relax before *I* have to hit him."

In minutes, not only was there someone working on the impromptu baby shower for the couple, but food had been ordered, drinks were being handed out, and they had information on how Sonny and the baby were doing. David came into the house with Josh, carrying a huge box each.

"I was hoping it would come tomorrow, but this might be better." With a cut along the tape, he opened one of the boxes up and handed Adrian his book. "I want Dylan to read the dedication. I wrote it for her grandda. But I have ordered everyone else a book. My first book about a real life history, and it comes out today—on my daughter's birthday. I could not be happier than I am right at this minute, Adrian."

The dedication was read aloud by Dylan. "To Mr. Bailey Hutchinson, my hero. Without your profound help, this book would not have been possible. The pictures inside are because you had the foresight to keep them. And your memories—some I shared, some I am keeping as a treasure in my heart—are here as well. Bailey, you were a wonderful human being, and I hope that someday I have the good fortune to see you again in the afterlife. Thank you for being my friend."

When Dylan started to cry, David looked at Evan. When he held his wife and shrugged, Dylan gave him a thumbs up while sobbing quietly with her face buried in Evan's chest. David smiled and hugged them both. Adrian left the room. He had to hold onto his own emotions for a moment.

"I've been thinking." He found Mason sitting in a chair out on the deck, where he'd been headed. Adrian asked her what it was she'd been thinking about. "I've been a cat a few times around the yard, usually when I'm feeling particularly lonely. But I'd really like to run with you. Now. Evan said it would be a while before the baby comes, and I need this."

"What's wrong? Not that I have a problem running with you. I've been thinking about it as well. But what makes you need it now?" He knelt down to be at her level. "Honey, what is it?"

"I have nothing to do." He wasn't sure what she meant, so didn't say anything. "I mean, before all this, I had a job, something to go to daily. Now I just sit around the house and play on the computer. I go out with your sisters—who I love, by the way. But I have nothing that I can call my own."

"You miss having a purpose." She nodded, and he could see the tears forming in her eyes. "I was going to suggest that you help out with the campaign, but Henry said that would tie you up and keep you from making appearances with me. But I do have some projects that I think you can do. Something that'll be needed more so when we're out."

"A pretty cling on?" He laughed. "You don't think I'm pretty? Well, that sucks. I thought you enjoyed the entirety of me."

"Oh, I do. Especially when you're naked. No, I was just thinking of you standing by me and not saying a word. That is not what I want at all. Nor, and I love you for this, do I think that it's something that you could do. You're more of a get it done kind of clinger. And that is perfect for what I need from you."

They talked for about an hour. Then when she stood up, he watched her shift from her beautiful self to her cat. Adrian knew that she'd be beautiful, but she was a gorgeous cat. And she was a black and white tiger.

I had to look it up to see how odd I was. But I'm not, not really. There have been sightings of my sort of tiger all over the world. And they believe that it's a mutation in the DNA from when I was born. Or, in this case, I'm assuming, when I was made. Did your family have a black and white tiger in the family line? He nodded. *Are you so disgusted with me or what?*

"Speechless is more like it. I knew all along that you'd be special, but just how special is beyond words. Christ, Mason, you're gorgeous. And yes, we have one in our line that is just like you. I'm going to go and get her so that she can see you. For a very long time, Aunt Bea wouldn't run with us because she thought herself ugly. I'd like for her to see you." Mason said that was fine with her, so long as they ran later. "You can count on that."

Aunt Bea was working on a crossword puzzle when he found her. She wasn't the normal grand aunt. She didn't knit, nor did she join any flower or tea parties. Aunt Bea drank liquor, enjoyed loud music, and kept to herself. She had told him once that she enjoyed the company of smart people, and that was why she enjoyed her own company. He hadn't got that until now.

Taking her outside, Adrian noticed that Mason had hidden herself. When he called for her, telling her that they were back, she came around the corner of the house walking like she'd been a cat her entire life. Then Mason rubbed her head on Aunt Bea's leg.

"Oh, child. You're beautiful." Aunt Bea got down on her knees and they bonded, putting their heads together as a way of greeting as cats. "I thought never to see one like me, ever. But you, you're nothing like me. I love you and your tiger, Mason. You've made an old woman very happy right now."

I love you too, Aunt Bea. They sat there, talking between themselves while Adrian watched. It was wonderful to see the two of them together. Aunt Bea seemed to be having a good deal of fun. *We're going for a run. Would you like to join us?*

"Oh no, child. Not today. But I think that I'd love to join you sometime. Just to feel the soil beneath my feet again." Aunt Bea smiled as she stood up. "You have given this old woman hope. Something that I've been missing for a while now. Thank you both."

Adrian had been excluded from their conversation, and he was glad for it. Whatever had been said between them had been just that, between them. When Aunt Bea kissed him on the cheek and went into the house, Adrian stood up and shifted to his plain old ordinary orange and black tiger. At least, that was how he felt right now.

Mason took off first. He could tell that she'd been practicing, like she'd said. He knew other made tigers that had to learn not just the basics, like walking, but how to hide when necessary, how to blend into the surrounding area. Mason was a natural.

I wish we had more time. He did, but they had the rest of their lives to play together. He'd not realized how much he'd needed this until he was chasing scents and running after Mason. *You're like a big kitten, aren't you? I bet if there were butterflies around, you'd be jumping up and down trying to catch one.*

Of course I would. So will you. It's not easy to curb that sort of fun. Besides, I think that our cats need a little play time too. How are you feeling now? She said she always felt better as a cat. *I know what you mean. But it's been hard for me to get away just to relax. It'll be harder still to do this when we're in the White House. If we make it there.*

You having doubts, Adrian? He hadn't thought so until just this minute, and told her that. *Tell me what it is you've been thinking. I'm not going to push you into anything or even try to talk you out of it. But you must have reasons.*

I do, but they seem so small in comparison to what I can do if I just stay here. She asked him what he meant. *I've been enjoying all the ideas of going to the White House, running the country. But I've also – I think, at least – made a huge difference right here. We're getting more jobs for the entire state. I've been working with other governors on some of the projects that we have started. Even the small ones of simply planting flowers and other vegetation for the small creatures that need us.*

Mason came and laid down beside him. *What makes you think you couldn't do that in the White House? And again, this is not me trying to talk you into it, but just asking as sort of the other side.*

I guess it's more personal for me here. She nodded and laid her head on his paw. *I can actually see what the progress is. I get to sit and talk to people that I might not be able to there. Like I said, this, here in this position, is more one on one for me.*

To be honest with you, I feel the same way. And we'd never get to do this, no matter what we might like to think. He said that there was that as well. *It's up to you, Adrian. You know that I will be right there with you with any decision you make. But, I'd like to point one thing out. You can always go to the White House later. It doesn't have to be now. Correct?*

Adrian laughed. *I honestly never thought of that. I swear, Mason, you are the best thing in the world for me. A balm when I need it, the best sexual partner in the world, and you tell me not what I want to hear but what I need to hear. I love you so very much.*

She's here. The call out had them both standing up. They could both hear the emotion in David's voice. *Oh guys, she's the most beautiful baby in the entire world. She looks just like her momma.*

~*~

Adrian was gone for the morning to talk to his brothers about the conversation that Mason and he had yesterday. Just as she was pulling up some of the projects that she'd gotten from Adrian this morning, a noise, just a slight cry like that of a baby, startled her into going to find out what it was. Mason stood very still when she saw the woman.

"She was hurting her." Mason just nodded. "I had to save her, you see. If I hadn't, she would have kept on hurting her."

"I'm glad then that you saved her. May I have a look at the baby?" She didn't relinquish her, but she did pull the blanket back enough for her to see the bright red hand prints on the baby's buttock. "Where did you get her?"

"At the other house." She looked around. "I don't know where I am. I was being hurt too, but I got away. Now I don't know where I am. Can you help us?"

"I can. Why don't we go to the living room and you can warm up? You also need to have a doctor look at your feet, I'm afraid." The woman shied away from her when she mentioned the doctor. "Evan is my brother-in-law and a good doctor. But I promise you, if he hurts either of you, I will kill him for you."

The woman laughed, and Mason reached out to Sonny. *I have little Beatrice, Sonny. She's safe and unharmed. She's here at my house. A woman said she was being abused and took her.* Sonny sobbed and said that she'd only just noticed that the baby was gone, and the nanny was unconscious. *The woman that has her, she showed me handprints on Beatrice's butt. And so you know, they're not from the woman that has her.*

I'm coming over right now. I don't know whether to be grateful or angry at this point.

In a few minutes not only was Sonny at her home, but Evan had come to look at the woman too. Sonny walked slowly to the woman. "Hello. That's Beatrice, my daughter. Mason said that you saved her for me. What's your name?"

It clearly upset her that she didn't know her name. It didn't seem to matter at the moment. The stranger handed the baby over to Sonny, but didn't move all that far from them. When Sonny sat down on the couch, so did the woman. Evan sat on the floor in front of her.

"You've come a long way, haven't you?" The woman said she didn't know, but she was very hungry. "I'm sure we can get you something to eat. What would you like? Mason has the greatest cook I know. She's the best at making grilled cheese."

"That would be good. And tomato soup too. That's what my mommy feeds me at home sometimes. She's going to be worried, isn't she?"

When Mason went to ask Doreen for the soup and sandwich, she wondered what they should do. Mason thought about calling the police, but that might upset the woman more than Evan coming to see her. She wasn't harming anyone. Mason knew that she was suffering from dementia, but how badly, she wasn't sure—end stage, she'd bet.

Going back to the living room, she saw that Sonny was nursing the baby with the woman watching on. Evan had had someone bring him a small tub of water so that he could soak the woman's feet.

"Do you know Nate?" No one answered the woman until Evan nodded. "He's a good friend of the woman that plays in my mommy's shed. There are some pretty horses there. Do you like horses, Doctor?"

"I do. We have some here. My family used to raise them when I was younger. We've sort of gotten out of that now." Evan looked at her. "Mason, do you think this is the family that Nate was telling us about? If so, she has come a very long way."

Mason said she'd talk to Nate and ask him about her. But as soon as he answered his cell phone, she knew that not only was this the family, but the woman had traveled from the Dayton area.

"I'm sorry, Mason, I have a friend of mine missing." Mason described the woman with her. "Oh thank...she's there? With you? Christ, she has been missing for a week, and we've been searching for her since. Her name is Jaclyn Hershey. Her mom is Elizabeth, but everyone around here just calls her Grannie. She has a daughter, Shadow, the artist I was telling you about. I'm going to tell them right now where she is. Oh, Mason, I'm so glad she found you instead of some crazy person. I forgot, she has dementia. She remembers some things, but not a great deal. I'll be there in a few hours. Thank you so much for calling me."

In a few minutes, her phone rang again. The picture that came up was of Nate, but it wasn't him that spoke when she answered it. The younger woman, Shadow was her name, asked about fifty questions before she took a breath and allowed Mason to answer.

"Slow down your grill, Shadow." The woman started crying. "Your mom is fine, I promise you. My brother-in-law, Evan, is looking her over now. Her feet are in poor shape, as she had no shoes on. And she's had a couple of grilled cheese sandwiches, as well as some soup. We're taking very good care of her."

"My grannie and I are coming to you. We've been frantic looking for her. I thought my uncle took her to prove a point, but he's in jail on something else. I don't know how she got out." Mason didn't tell her about the marks on her wrists, nor the burns from rope around her ankles. Shadow was stressed out enough. "If Nate asks, no, I'm not driving. Grannie is."

"I'll make sure that I tell him. Shadow, is there anything else we should know? I mean, does she have any allergies?" Shadow asked the other person with her. "Your grannie, I take it."

"Yes, she's my rock since Mom got.... It's fine, Mrs. Whitfield. We'll be there in a few hours. And no, Mom doesn't have any allergies. But she has a very sweet tooth. With chocolate. So be aware."

Jacklyn feet were bandaged up now, and Evan had given her a tetanus shot after making a quick call to the daughter. Then he looked at her other wounds—not as bad as her feet, but just as worrisome. Putting her to bed to rest, Sonny kindly gave her one of Beatrice's stuffed animals.

Coming out of the bedroom, Mason saw Tanner.

"My lady. I'm sorry that I've not been around much, but other duties have taken my spare time away. But I have spoken to Nate—good pack leader, by the way—and he has had the family pull to the side of the road. With your permission I will bring them both here, and Nate will drive their car the rest of the way."

She told him that was fine with her. Then he disappeared. In less than a minute, a younger version of the woman sleeping was standing in front of her.

"Shadow?" She nodded, holding onto the wall as she did. "Yes, I'm to understand that it sort of takes a bit out of you to move like that. Come, your mom is resting. If you'd like something to eat or drink, you only have to pick up the phone there and press three. We're here to help you in any way possible."

She opened the door just in time to greet the other woman.

She too looked like a version of the woman in the bed, and Mason told her the same thing. When she closed the door behind them, they were both crying quietly. Mason made her way downstairs to see about getting some extras laid in for the other two.

"Just some sandwich things for now, Doreen. Later if they want, we can sit down and have a meal together. And I doubt that either one of them brought anything to wear or such. I'll have to talk to someone about that." She said that Sonny had taken care of that. "I don't know what that might mean, but that'll be great too."

Remembering that she needed to let Adrian know what was going on and that he was going to find a few strangers in their home, she contacted him and he laughed. She asked him what was so funny.

You. You certainly found yourself something to bide your time, didn't you? She told him he was an ass. *I am at that. And after talking to my brothers, you and I have to have a conversation again. They think that we're doing the right thing. You have no idea how much that has taken off my shoulders.*

I wish you had said something sooner, Adrian. You even sound less stressed out. I love you, and want only the best for you. He said he knew that as well. *All right. I'm going to see about organizing a nice dinner. Have some of the family over that has been helping me out today. That all right with you?*

Yes. And Doreen told me this morning before I left that she needed to make some big meals, that we need to have the family over more. She's a find, I tell you. And I could die a happy man when she makes those Danish sweet rolls for me. Mason knew that Adrian had begged for them last night, and had had enough to take with him this morning, leaving her one of them. *Oh, before I forget, I got a call from Bryant Green, the art critic. He's going to make a trip to see Shadow's art work. I'd not tell her if I were you. She's very touchy about it, Nate told me.*

All right. Wouldn't it be a hoot if she turns out to be Blake's mate? They both laughed. *Oh well, I have stuff to get going before you get home. I love you, Adrian.*

And I love you very much, Mason. I'll be home in a couple of hours. Hold dinner for me, please? Doreen is making me chicken fried steaks with mashed potatoes and green beans. Mason told him that he was a hog. *No, just a man that likes comfort food. I'll see you soon.*

After making sure that the women were set, she made her way to the office. She felt better than she had the first time she sat down here earlier. Now, she felt like she had a purpose, and was glad that she and Adrian had talked.

Before You Go...

HELP AN AUTHOR

write a review

THANK YOU!

Share your voice and help guide other readers to these wonderful books. Even if it's only a line or two your reviews help readers discover the author's books so they can continue creating stories that you'll love. Login to your favorite retailer and leave a review. Thank you.

Kathi Barton, winner of the Pinnacle Book Achievement award as well as a best-selling author on Amazon and All Romance books, lives in Nashport, Ohio with her husband Paul. When not creating new worlds and romance, Kathi and her husband enjoy camping and going to auctions. She can also be seen at county fairs with her husband who is an artist and potter.

Her muse, a cross between Jimmy Stewart and Hugh Jackman, brings her stories to life for her readers in a way that has them coming back time and again for more. Her favorite genre is paranormal romance with a great deal of spice. You can visit Kathi online and drop her an email if you'd like. She loves hearing from her fans. aaronskiss@gmail.com.

Follow Kathi on her blog: http://kathisbartonauthor.blogspot.com/

Printed in Great Britain
by Amazon